"I don't think this will work out, Haley."

Haley stared at Matthew. "I'm really sorry for letting Lizzie—I mean Elizabeth—miss her nap."

"It's not just that," Matthew countered. "It's *everything*."

She waited for him to list her infractions, but he didn't, so she could only guess that there were many. "I know I'm a bit... unconventional..."

"To say the least."

Haley swallowed. "I can do better. I'll do things your way. I need this job." She needed Elizabeth, too. It was probably pitiful to admit it, but she never felt more valued than she did by a child who needed her care.

"I'm sorry, Haley. I don't think—"

"But I love her, Matthew."

He opened his mouth to say something, then closed it. Haley studied him, waiting. Had she said the one thing that would make a difference?

Books by Dana Corbit

Love Inspired

A Blessed Life
An Honest Life
A New Life
A Family for Christmas
"Child in a Manger"
On the Doorstep
Christmas in the Air
"Season of Hope"
A Hickory Ridge Christmas
Little Miss Matchmaker
Homecoming at Hickory Ridge
*An Unexpected Match

*Wedding Bell Blessings

DANA CORBIT

started telling "people stories" at about the same time she started forming words. So it came as no surprise when the Indiana native chose a career in journalism. As an award-winning newspaper reporter and features editor, she had the opportunity to share wonderful true-life stories with her readers. She left the workforce to be a homemaker, but the stories came home with her as she discovered the joy of writing fiction. Winner of the 2007 Holt Medallion competition for novel writing, Dana feels blessed to share the stories of her heart with readers.

Dana lives in southeast Michigan, where she balances the make-believe realm of her characters with her equally exciting real-life world as a wife, carpool coordinator for three athletic daughters and food supplier for two disinterested felines.

An Unexpected Match
Dana Corbit

Steeple
Hill®

Published by Steeple Hill Books™

STEEPLE HILL BOOKS

Steeple
Hill®

Recycling programs
for this product may
not exist in your area.

ISBN-13: 978-0-373-81422-0

AN UNEXPECTED MATCH

Copyright © 2009 by Dana Corbit Nussio

www.SteepleHill.com

Printed in U.S.A.

May the God of hope fill you with all joy and peace
in believing, so that by the power of the
Holy Spirit you may abound in hope.
—*Romans* 15:13

To my nieces Alyssa, Christine, Jennifer, Stephanie, Elizabeth, Margaret and Catherine, and nephews Joel, Matthew, Ethan and Eyan, some of whom already have been bitten by the writing bug. Never be afraid to tell the story of your heart. And to Mike Waltersdorf and the whole gang at Biggby Coffee in Novi, Michigan, for cheering me on while I was writing on deadline and making sure the vanilla lattes were nice and hot.

Chapter One

"Is there a Haley Scott here?"

Haley glanced through the storm door at the package carrier before opening the latch, letting in some of the frigid March wind.

"That's me, but not for long."

The blank stare the man gave her as he stood on the porch of her mother's new house only made Haley smile. In fifty-one hours and twenty-nine minutes, her name would be changing. Her life, as well, but she couldn't allow herself to think about that now.

She wouldn't attribute her sudden shiver to anything but the cold, either. Not with a bridal fitting to endure, embossed napkins to pick up and a caterer to call. Too many details, too little time—and certainly no time for her to entertain her silly cold feet.

"Then this is for you."

Practiced at this procedure after two days back in her Markston, Indiana hometown, Haley reached out both arms to accept a bridal gift, but the carrier turned and deposited an overnight letter package in just one of her hands. Haley stared down at the Michigan return address of her fiancé, Tom Jeffries.

"Strange way to send a wedding present," she murmured.

The man grunted and shoved an electronic signature device at her, waiting until she scrawled her name.

As soon as she closed the door, Haley returned to the living room and yanked the tab on the envelope. From it, she withdrew a single sheet of folded notebook paper.

Something inside her suggested that she should sit down to read it, so she lowered herself into a floral side chair. Hesitating before she unfolded the note, she glanced at the far wall where wedding gifts in pastel-colored paper were stacked. Her stomach tightened as she read each handwritten word.

"*Best?* He signed it *best?*" Her voice cracked as the paper fluttered to the floor. She was sure she should be sobbing or collapsing in a heap, but she only felt numb as she stared down at the offensive piece of paper.

The letter that had changed everything.

"Best what?" Trina Scott asked as she padded into the room with fuzzy striped socks on her feet. "Sweetie?"

Haley lifted her gaze to meet her mother's and could see concern etched between her carefully tweezed brows.

"What's the matter?" Trina shot a glance toward the foyer, her chin-length brown hair swinging past her ear as she did it. "Did I just hear someone at the door?"

Haley tilted her head to indicate the sheet of paper on the floor. "It's from Tom. He called off the wedding."

"What?" Trina began but then brushed her hand through the air twice as if to erase the question. "That's not the most important thing right now, is it?"

Haley stared at her mother. A little pity wouldn't have been out of place here. Instead of offering any, Trina snapped up the letter and began to read. When she finished, she sat on the cream-colored sofa opposite Haley's chair.

"I don't approve of his methods." She shook the letter to emphasize her point. "And I always thought the boy didn't have enough good sense to come out of the rain, but I have to agree with him on this one. You two aren't right for each other."

Haley couldn't believe her ears. Okay, Tom

wouldn't have been the partner Trina Scott would have chosen for her youngest daughter if Trina's grand matchmaking scheme hadn't gone belly up. Still, Haley hadn't realized how strongly her mother had disapproved of her choice.

"No sense being upset about my opinion now," Trina told her. "I kept praying that you'd make the right decision, but I guess Tom made it for you. Now we have to get busy. There are a lot of calls to make."

Suddenly, tears that had been slow in coming were pouring down Haley's cheeks. Humiliation made her skin burn. How could she stand in front of the church and announce that her wedding had been canceled? But her problems went beyond embarrassment over a ceremony that wouldn't happen and gifts that would need to be returned.

"Oh, Mom. What am I going to do? I quit my job. I gave up my apartment. I was supposed to move into Tom's place right after the wedding."

"You'll stay here until you find another job and another place to live. You weren't planning to always work in—what was it this time—that hospital records department, anyway, were you?"

Haley shrugged. She couldn't focus on her distant future when all she could think about was that the day after tomorrow should have been her wedding day. "Wait. When were Jenna and Caroline coming in?"

As she asked, a key turned in the lock, ending all hope that she would be able to catch her sisters before they boarded their flights to Indianapolis. Jenna burst through the door, whistling the tune of "Chapel of Love." She pulled the smallish suitcase she used in her job as an airline attendant behind her. A less-experienced traveler, Caroline followed her in, dragging a heavy, wheeled suitcase.

Still humming as she jogged into the living room, Jenna paused when she saw Haley. The song died on her lips.

"What's wrong *now?*" Jenna visibly braced herself, just as she had a year before when Haley had met her flight to tell her their father had died of a heart attack.

Caroline gripped her hands together. "What is it?"

"Everything's fine," their mother told them. "Except there's been a change of plans. There won't be a wedding this weekend after all."

"What happened?" Jenna asked.

"Tom sent a letter to call off the wedding," their mother explained.

Caroline's eyes widened. "A 'Dear Jane' letter?"

"Two days before the wedding?" Jenna chimed.

"Ladies." Trina held up her hand. "Haley has received some difficult news, and she's going to need our help."

Haley shifted in her seat and waited. Even if their mother wasn't the touchy-feely kind of mom who kissed scraped knees, her sisters would come through with the hugs she needed. As if on cue, they rushed to her and sandwiched her between them. But before Haley could sink into their embrace, Jenna pulled her head back.

"At least one of you came to your senses," Jenna said with a grin.

Caroline was smiling as well when she released Haley. "If he'd waited much longer, we would have been forced to make the announcement at the church like a cheesy movie-of-the-week."

Haley closed her eyes and opened them again, convinced she was in some alternate reality. Where was her real family that should have been furious on her behalf? If they were on camera for some video prank show, she wished the host would just jump out and let her in on the joke because right now, none of it was funny.

"If you all believed I shouldn't get married, why didn't you say something?"

"We did," Caroline said. "Many times. You wouldn't listen."

Jenna held her hands wide. "Remember all of the tag-team phone calls where Caroline and I said that no one should get married until she's thirty and where we cited all the newest divorce statistics?"

Come to think of it... Haley shook her head. "I thought you just didn't want me to be the first one to marry."

Her sisters turned pitying glances her way, and those humiliated her more than their jokes.

Their mother was already lacing up the white leather sneakers she called "errand shoes" when Haley turned back to her.

"Okay, there are a lot of details that need to be dealt with to un-plan a wedding," Trina said.

Un-plan. Haley rolled the sour word on her tongue. She'd liked the idea of having the first Scott wedding. Third-born children never had the opportunity to do *anything* first. Having the chance to be the first sister dumped just short of the ceremony wasn't what she'd had in mind.

Heat built behind her nose and eyes again, but she struggled to hold back tears. "You two don't need to stay here to take care of the details."

"Why not?" Jenna asked. "We already took vacation to spend some time here with Mom after the—I mean...after. And you know how hard it is to get Caroline to take any time off from the mega mall. She would be back at work thirty minutes after her plane touched down at O'Hare."

"I would not." Caroline frowned since her workaholic tendencies were as much a source of family humor as Haley's frequent job changes. "Anyway, we're staying."

Jenna rubbed her hands together. "What's first?"

"I'll call Amy." Trina dug the cell phone from her purse and hit one of the speed dial numbers.

Haley winced. In any situation, it shouldn't have surprised her that her mother's first reaction was to phone her best friend, but Trina had more than knee-jerk reasons to make this call. Not only had Amy Warren been asked to join them downtown this afternoon for Haley's final bridal fitting, but she also was scheduled to make the wedding cake at her bakery, Amy's Elite Treats.

Haley asked herself again why she'd agreed to have the wedding in her hometown. Now her humiliation would double as she shared it with family friends. One in particular.

"May I speak to Amy?" Trina began as someone answered the line. "Oh, Matthew, is that you?"

That's the one. Haley squeezed her eyes shut. If there was one person Haley wished could miss the news flash about her suspended nuptials, it was Matthew Warren. He'd already witnessed one of her most embarrassing moments, and now he would have a front-row seat to another.

"Oh, the wedding," Trina continued, oblivious to her daughter's mortification. "That's why I called. Here, let me speak to your mother first."

First. Of course, Matthew Warren would need to hear the news of a canceled wedding second or at least third, behind the Reverend Leyton Boggs, who would have performed the ceremony. As part-time music minister at the Community Church of Markston, Matthew would be in the loop.

Haley stood and backed from the room, not wanting to hear the events rehashed. Jenna started to follow, but Haley shook her head to stop her.

"I just need to fix my makeup."

In the bathroom, Haley wiped trails of mascara from her face with a dampened tissue. She was still patting dry her cheeks when someone rapped on the door.

"Sweetie, are you all right?" Trina pushed open the door and stuck her head inside. "Amy said she was sorry to hear the news. She canceled the cake order. Too bad the bridal shop won't be able to do that for the dress."

"Oh." Haley closed her eyes, pinching the bridge of her nose. "I hadn't even thought about that yet." What she would do with a silk bridal gown with an empire waist, she had no idea. Maybe make white silk bathroom curtains?

"Matthew said he was sorry, too."

Haley lowered her hand and opened her eyes, her cheeks growing warm. "That was nice of him."

Her mother studied her face as if deciding whether to tell her more. Haley would have assured her that nothing could surprise her now, but then Trina spoke again.

"Matthew also told me to tell you if there's anything he can do to help, you should just ask."

Matthew Warren jumped at the sound of the doorbell, narrowly missing slicing his finger in the same julienne style as the carrots on his mother's cutting board.

"I'll get it." Four-year-old Elizabeth climbed down from the stool where she'd been *helping* by playing in the sudsy dishwater. She raced across the room.

Matthew caught his daughter before she reached the swinging kitchen door and hoisted her into his arms. "I don't think so, young lady. You know only grown-ups are supposed to answer the door. What if it's a stranger?"

"Those aren't strangers," his mother supplied, patting her short silver hair. "They're our guests."

"Well, about that..." He glanced at the kitchen door, feeling the same nervous tension he experienced whenever he met new clients at his law practice. "Did I mention that this dinner is a bad idea?"

"About five times now."

"Haley's probably still reeling from the news. I doubt she's in the mood for socializing."

"Maybe not."

"And Elizabeth and I shouldn't be here, either. I have things I need to do. If I don't find a new sitter by Monday…"

Amy Warren stopped, planting her hands on her hips. "Matthew, we still have to eat."

The bell rang again. It was an unnecessary interruption to the dispute since Matthew had already lost.

"Daddy! The door." Elizabeth wiggled out of his arms and then grabbed his hand, pulling him from the kitchen.

"Coming," he called out as they hurried down the hall.

Tonight's dinner was still a bad idea, in his opinion. The whole thing felt like an ambush. He shouldn't have offered his help to Haley, either, when he was dealing with enough of his own problems. His mother's stubbornness over her dinner party irritated him, but everything had bugged him today since he'd made the mistake of answering his mother's cell phone while on his lunch hour.

In the foyer, he hesitated. He had no reason to be nervous. It had all happened a long time ago, and even then it hadn't been a big deal. Anyway, Haley probably had bigger things on her mind today than her adolescent crush that had ended in an embarrassing rejection. Shaking his head, he opened the door.

Trina Scott stood on the stoop, her gloved hand poised to knock. "Oh, there you are. I thought you were going to let us freeze out here."

Behind her, the older two Scott sisters stood in their heavy coats, their arms laden with food.

"Sorry about that," he said.

Elizabeth squeezed in front of him as he pushed open the storm door to let them inside. "Hi, Grandma Trina. Daddy and Grammy were arguing in the kitchen."

"Really?" Trina lifted an eyebrow as she leaned in to hug Matthew and then dropped a kiss on Elizabeth's head. She turned to her daughters. "Elizabeth needed something to call me, so Amy thought 'Grandma Trina' would be nice."

Matthew turned to the other women. "Hey, Jenna. Hey, Caroline. Where's Haley?"

Just as he spoke her name, the fourth guest appeared behind them, her face peering out from the hood of her parka. She opened the door and stepped inside.

"Hi, Haley. It's been a long time."

"Yes, it has."

Haley flicked her gaze his way as she removed her coat and handed it to him. She looked different, but he should have expected that. People tended to change after nine years. Her hair was blonder than he had remembered, and though she used to wear it long like her sisters, she'd cut it in a sassy shag style that reached just to her chin. It suited her, he decided.

"Who's she, Daddy?"

Matthew glanced down at the child tugging his arm and then looked back to Haley. "I guess you two haven't met." Of course, they hadn't. Her sisters had helped their mother move back to Markston a year before and had visited a few times since, but until now, Haley hadn't made the trip.

Instead of answering him, Haley crouched in front of his daughter and extended her hand. "Hello. I'm Haley."

"Call her Miss Haley," Matthew instructed.

Though the child could sometimes be shy with strangers, she bravely shot out her hand. "I'm Elizabeth."

"It's nice to meet you, Elizabeth." Haley shook the child's tiny hand.

Elizabeth tilted her head to the side and studied the woman still crouched before her. "You're pretty."

"Thanks. So are you." Haley stood again and toyed with the belt of her sweater.

Leave it to a four-year-old to state the obvious. Haley was an attractive woman, just like her sisters. Though "little Haley" had been a cute kid, the twenty-three-year-old had come into her own look as the rest of her face had finally caught up to those huge, bright blue eyes. The pretty, high cheekbones and generous lips were clearly Scott family traits.

Matthew stopped himself. What was he doing? He had no business noticing women. Particularly someone like Haley Scott. Someone like…

He looked away from her but not before she glanced back and caught him studying her. The color spreading on her cheeks suggested that she'd mistaken his curiosity for pity. Of course, she would think that on a day like today.

"So…" Caroline cast a frown his way. "Where's everyone else?"

"It's just us, I'm afraid," Amy Warren said as she emerged from the kitchen, wiping her hands on her apron.

"The guys aren't here?" Jenna looked disappointed. She and Dylan had always been the closest among the Warren-Scott children, but even they had lost contact over the last few years.

Amy Warren shook her head. "Dylan's at an optometry meeting in Chicago, and Logan has a date."

She cast a glance Matthew's way as if daring him to contradict his youngest brother's story. Somehow Matthew managed to keep a straight face. There were few nights when Logan *didn't* have a date, but none that couldn't have been rescheduled. Matthew had a better excuse than either of his brothers for not coming tonight—a child-care crisis—but, as usual, he was present and accounted for. Just once, he wished he could share the freedom from obligation his brothers enjoyed.

Trina Scott crossed the room to hug her best friend. "Thank you for inviting us." Like the elephant in the living room, she avoided mentioning the reason her daughters were in town in the first place.

"Here, let me take some of that food for you." Matthew reached for the casserole dish in Jenna's arms.

"Elizabeth will show us where the kitchen is," Jenna told him, though they could have found it blindfolded.

Elizabeth led Jenna and Caroline down the hall. Caught in some hushed conversation, the two mothers headed in the same direction, leaving Matthew and Haley standing alone in the entry. Haley had moved away from the door and was staring at a photo collage on the wall.

"We had a lot of good times back then," she said when he stood next to her.

"The best."

As Matthew tried to come up with something comforting to say, the impulse to touch her shoulder surprised him. Even if she'd had a lousy day, Haley was a grown woman now. She could take care of herself. His knight-in-shining-armor gear fit uncomfortably, and he doubted she would appreciate his need to protect, anyway.

At the sound of someone clearing her throat, Matthew glanced back at his mother and Mrs. Scott.

"What are you two just standing there for?" Amy asked. "Now get in the kitchen and help, or it'll be midnight before we eat."

"Many hands make light work," Trina added.

Her comment made him smile. How many times had Mrs. Scott or his mother said those same words while they were all staying at the beach condo in Hilton Head or in that mountain rental in Gatlinburg?

"After you, ladies." Matthew gestured gallantly.

"Just make sure you're right behind us," Trina said.

When he and Haley were alone again, Matthew paused, searching for the right words. Something wise, he hoped. Something that would make her feel better. But when he peeked at her, Haley was watching him.

The side of her mouth lifted. "You heard them. Now get to work."

"Yes, ma'am." He saluted, but he must have failed to hide his surprise that she'd played along with the old family game because Haley crossed her arms over her chest.

"I'm not made of blown glass, you know."

"Never said you were."

"Then stop looking at me like I'm about to shatter."

"I didn't mean to—"

She waved away his apology before he could finish it. "Forget it. I'm getting used to it. Everyone I've talked to today…even mom's new neighbors—they all feel sorry for me. It's a real blast."

"I can imagine."

"I always wondered what it would be like to be a celebrity." She moved her head back and forth, as if weighing her opinion. "It has a downside. Anyway, we'd better get in there before they send a search party."

Haley started down the hall, Matthew falling into step behind her. Outside the swinging kitchen door, he gave in to the earlier temptation and rested a hand on her shoulder. She stiffened but didn't shake away his hand.

"I'm sorry about…everything that happened," he said.

"Yeah, me, too. But what doesn't kill us makes us stronger."

She had to be speaking of today and the loss of the person she'd cared about enough to consider making her husband. Matthew understood that. The hurt he'd played a part in had been a long time ago and nothing compared to what she'd experienced today.

Still, he'd been apologizing for both.

Chapter Two

As Haley scanned the length of the Warren family's formal dining table, she felt warm for the first time all day. Yes, a few of the maple dining chairs were empty, and a pint-size newcomer sat cross-legged in another, but the place offered the same comfort she had remembered.

She'd always loved coming here, hearing her mother and Mrs. Warren tell the same stories that never lost their sparkle. There was stability in the sameness, comfort in the familiarity.

Even seeing Matthew again hadn't felt as awkward as she'd expected, so her excuse for staying away from Scott-Warren gatherings seemed silly now. Matthew had always been a decent boy, the one who'd insisted that she and Logan be allowed to play board games with the older kids. She should have known he wouldn't grow into the type of man who would embarrass her over the past. That sweet little girl across the table, the one with two sandy-brown braids and caramel-colored eyes that mirrored her father's, reminded her that Matthew had more important things on his mind these days.

Though Matthew had changed some since the last time she'd seen him, she still would have recognized that baby face anywhere. At twenty-eight, he'd filled out his lanky frame, and the peach fuzz that used to dust his upper lip and chin had been replaced by a five o'clock shadow, two shades darker than his hair. He probably chose those mod-shaped glasses rather than contacts to make him look older.

"Remember the time that Haley fed soap shavings to Logan's fish?" Mrs. Warren was saying when Haley returned to the conversation.

"Poor Crunch," Caroline said and made a sad face.

"Am I ever going to live that down?" Haley frowned. "Who names a fish *Crunch* anyway?"

Seated next to her father, Elizabeth looked up from the pile of peas she was scattering on her plate. "Miss Haley killed Crunch?"

Everyone laughed at the horror in the child's voice before her grandma explained that Crunch had survived his sudsy ordeal. "You and Logan always were like oil and water whenever you were together."

"Didn't bode well for your old matchmaking scheme," Caroline chimed. She must have realized it was poor timing for one of her dry side comments because she met Haley's gaze and winced.

Trina and Amy missed that exchange as they grinned at each other across the table.

"Wow, *the plan*," Trina said, shaking her head. "We haven't talked about that in years."

"Matched sets!" The two mothers exclaimed the words in unison, and with equally precise timing, the three Scott sisters and the lone Warren brother groaned.

Haley rolled her eyes. She should have known that even on a day like today the two moms would reminisce about their silly idea to arrange marriages among their six children. Their plan had been a running family joke, but it was far less funny today.

"It was worth a try, anyway," Amy said. "Since your mother and I were pregnant together for at least a few months three different times, and she had the girls while I had the boys, we figured we might have a shot for at least one proper matchup."

"God made it easy by giving us even pairs," Trina supplied. "Two oldest, two middle and two youngest."

"I sure messed that up then, didn't I?"

This wasn't the first sardonic comment Matthew had made tonight, but this time he didn't get a laugh. Jenna cleared her throat, while the others took renewed interest in their food. Even living in Michigan, Haley had heard all about Matthew's brief marriage to his college girlfriend who deserted him and their infant daughter.

"Messed up what, Daddy?"

"Just a game," he assured her. "Now eat your peas."

Amy tugged one of her granddaughter's braids. "Sure, it was just a game." She looked farther down the table to her son. "But two moms could dream, couldn't they?"

"Moms never stop dreaming," Trina said. The meaningful look she gave first to Matthew and then Caroline left no doubt that she hadn't given up on their matchmaking plan, especially where those two were concerned. Caroline's cheeks were pink as she concentrated too intently on her roast beef.

Haley had a strange impulse to raise her hand and announce, "Hey, this is supposed to be about me." If their mothers were going to start match-making again, at least they could have waited for another day. Not the day of her broken engagement.

Anyway, if they only knew. She'd never told them then, and she certainly didn't plan to now, but at one time, one of the Scott sisters had longed for a matchup with a certain Warren brother. At the memory of her crush from long ago, Haley coughed into her napkin. Her cheeks burned. She felt fourteen again, the embarrassing images repeating in her mind like a love story performed in a *Three Stooges* episode.

"You okay?" Matthew asked when her gaze darted his way again. His eyebrows were drawn together above the frames of his glasses.

She nodded. The others studied her with the same concern they'd focused on her most of the night. If they'd known what she'd been thinking about just then, they really would have been worried. She had no business ruminating on an adolescent crush when the real love of her life had deserted her only hours before. It just went to show how muddled her thoughts had become tonight.

"Is anyone ready for dessert?" Matthew asked, breaking the silence.

Elizabeth shot a hand into the air. "I am. I am." She leaned in and announced in a stage whisper, "Do you want some, Miss Haley? Grammy said it's chocolate cake."

Of course, it would be cake. Even before opening her own bakery, Amy Warren had made all the scrumptious desserts for their gatherings. The only difference now was she brought them home in a box. Amy hurried into the kitchen, with Elizabeth trailing behind her to help and probably sample the frosting.

Haley's mother stood and started stacking

dishes. "If all this had happened one day later, we would have had an even bigger dessert. Amy's staff would have already started on the cake, so we could have split a three-tier wedding cake seven ways."

"I would have taken that challenge," Matthew said. "Imagine that, a baker's son who still loves wedding cake."

Haley cleared her throat to get their attention. "Sure glad my sad story is a punch line for everyone." She frowned first at her mother and then at Matthew. "Why didn't you just keep tip-toeing around the subject? You were doing a good job of it."

"Because you need to talk about the wedding," Trina insisted. "It'll be easier to heal if you do."

"I don't want to talk about it, Mom." *Not here. Not in front of these people.*

Matthew spread his hands wide. "Then you don't have to talk about it, at least not until you're ready."

Trina blew out a frustrated breath, but she nodded. "Fine. When you're ready."

Amy picked that moment to return with the cake, her assistant following closely behind. "Now everyone had better take a piece, or I'll be offended."

Despite the warning, Jenna attempted to decline but ended up with a big piece in front of her anyway. Soon appreciative murmurs filled the room.

Haley studied the people around her as they ate. How many times had they gathered around a table just like this one, sharing food and their lives? These people were like her extended family. They'd been there for her during the trials of her childhood, and they were there for her now, waiting to talk about her life-changing day until she was ready. Maybe she could talk about it after all.

"Boy, it's a good thing there's not going to be a wedding." Haley waited until all those surprised faces turned her way before she continued. "After this dinner, I never would have fit in my wedding gown."

"You're not getting married?" Elizabeth asked.

Matthew sent a wary look his daughter's way. Of course, no one had thought to tell Elizabeth.

"No, sweetie," Haley said. "We canceled the wedding."

"But why?"

Haley shrugged, uncertain how to explain to a child what she didn't know for sure herself. "My fiancé decided he didn't want to marry me."

Elizabeth sat straighter in her seat and crossed her arms. "He was mean not to marry someone nice like you."

They all laughed at the child's summation of the situation, except Haley, who managed a smile. She wasn't ready to join in the laughter, but she didn't feel the need to sob on the floor, either. It was a start.

With the taboo subject of the canceled ceremony now on the table, the women began dividing up their assignments for the next day. Jenna would meet with the florist who had to cancel a whole order of white roses, while Haley took on the bridal storeowner and Caroline faced off with the caterer, dealing with cancellation policies. Haley's mother had volunteered for the task of phoning all the guests.

Caroline looked up from the notebook she'd pulled from her purse, with the first two pages already detailing the next day's chores. "Too bad Mom doesn't have a best friend who is owner of one of these other businesses."

"We did get special treatment there." Trina turned to Amy. "I don't know how to thank you for returning the deposit."

Amy waved off her friend's thanks. "What are friends for? You might recoup some of your money on the dresses, too, if the bridal shop owner agrees to sell them on consignment. It's good when couples can reclaim some of their costs, so they'll be able to focus their attention on what to do next."

Haley could feel Mrs. Warren's gaze on her, but she couldn't bring herself to look at her. Beyond tomorrow's chores, she didn't know what she would do next. She realized that she needed to carve out a new life for herself now, a focused life, but how could she find it when she didn't know what she wanted?

"Okay, what's my job?" Matthew asked as he leaned forward, bracing his forearms on the table.

"Hang around and nod your head a lot," Jenna supplied.

Caroline looked up from her list. "You could check off chores on the list while the rest of us do the jobs."

"Or," Amy paused for effect before adding, "you could tag along while Caroline talks with the caterer."

Matthew shot a frown his mother's way, but then he turned back to the others.

"What is this? I thought you were all evolved, twenty-first-century women, and here you are applying a double standard by saying a man wouldn't know his way around wedding plans. I'll have you know that I plan the music for all the weddings at our church, and no one ever complains."

"Then what do *you* want to do?" Jenna asked.

"I don't know." He hesitated, as if he'd just realized what he'd gotten himself into. "I can handle anything as long as it doesn't involve frilly dresses or makeup."

Caroline glanced down at her list and then at Matthew again. "You could help repackage the gifts for return."

He turned to Haley. "You have to return the gifts?"

"That's how it works," Haley said.

"She doesn't have to return mine." Caroline crossed her arms over her chest. "Single women can use blenders, too."

Matthew was grinning over Caroline's feminist perspective when he turned back to her youngest sister. "You don't need to open Caroline's gift since she gave away the surprise. It's a blender."

"It is not," Caroline insisted, but everyone laughed again, anyway.

Haley even chuckled this time, the light feeling in her chest offering another surprise in a day chock-full of them. She'd planned to be at her rehearsal dinner tomorrow night. *Surprise.* She'd expected that the details in her life would be neatly in order by Saturday afternoon. *Surprise.* And now she'd discovered that with the support of family and these friends, she might someday have more reasons to laugh again.

The two families were working together to clear away dishes as they'd done so many times over the years when Amy Warren cornered her son in the kitchen.

"I have a better idea for something you can do to help Haley," she told him.

He lowered an armload of half-empty platters

on the counter. "What's that? And don't tell me it's by going out with a certain sister of hers, either."

"I have no idea what you're talking about."

"Mother," he said in a warning tone.

"We'll worry about that later." Glancing at the door separating the kitchen from the dining room, she gestured for him to come closer to the sink. She spoke in hushed tones. "You can kill two birds with one stone. You need a child-care provider, at least a temporary one, and Haley needs a job."

Matthew was shaking his head before the plan was out of her mouth. He felt badly for only thinking of his own problems when Haley was having a crisis, and he'd wanted to help her in some way, but this wasn't it. "You're not serious."

"Of course, I am."

"But this is Haley Scott we're talking about." Haley, whose résumé was too long to fit on one page, and not in a good way. Haley, who switched college majors and jobs as often as other people changed clothes. But he said only, "I don't think that's a good idea. And besides, I still have a few candidates left to interview."

Amy shrugged as she rinsed dishes and loaded them in the dishwasher. "Up to you."

"Yes, it is."

His mother clearly disagreed with him, but as Elizabeth's father, it was up to him to decide who should provide care for her. What kind of father would he be to trust his child to someone as flighty as Haley? He couldn't even understand why his mother had suggested it, except that Haley was her best friend's daughter.

His obligation was to his own daughter, whose needs he would always put ahead of his own or anyone else's. Elizabeth deserved better than a child-care provider who might desert her without looking back. Might do exactly what his ex-wife had done.

"She isn't Stacey, you know," his mother said.

Matthew blinked. His mother was bringing out the big guns if she was mentioning his ex. He'd declared that name off-limits, and usually his family abided by that rule. Before he could call out his mother for breaking the rule, though, Jenna pushed through the door, carrying an armful of dishes. Haley followed right behind her, but she only had dishes in one hand because his daughter was holding the other.

Matthew glanced surreptitiously at his mother, who caught his attention and grinned. He started shoving dishes into the dishwasher, hoping the others hadn't overheard their earlier conversation.

"I was just telling Haley that when I get back from the florist tomorrow, we can go shopping for some new outfits," Jenna said. "There are so many cute styles for spring."

"Jenna, I don't think—"

"Aw, come on. It'll be fun."

Their mother and Caroline entered the kitchen, stopping just inside the door.

"You know...shopping therapy," Jenna continued. "Haley will want to look her best when she gets back out there."

"Back out there?"

The dread in Haley's voice couldn't be missed. She didn't sound anywhere near ready to be *out there* again. Matthew knew what that was like, and he could also relate to times when relatives' well-meaning *help* felt too much like pressure.

"Shopping therapy might work for some, but are you sure that's what your sister wants to do?" Matthew turned to Haley. "Haley, what *do* you want to do?"

"That is the question of the day." Haley shook her head, appearing overwhelmed with the thought. "Haley Scott, what do you plan to do with the rest of your life?" For the last, she took on a game show announcer's voice.

"I'm not talking about the rest of your life. Just tomorrow." Matthew had been searching for a way to help, and now it seemed obvious: He could give her something to do to take her mind off her problems. She probably needed a temporary distraction even if he doubted she would accept that distraction from him. They hadn't exactly parted on the best of terms the last time they'd seen each other.

"Oh, tomorrow. I hadn't really thought about it."

"Well, I have an idea if you need one. Something fun."

"Like what?"

Her answer surprised him since he expected an automatic "no." He cleared his throat before giving his pitch. "I'm chaperoning a youth group road rally at church, and I thought you might like to tag along."

"Sounds to me as if they're short on volunteers."

"No. That's not it," he began, but he stopped when the side of her mouth lifted. "I just thought— Anyway, it's a photo scavenger hunt, and I'm one of the drivers."

Matthew placed a few more glasses in the top rack of the dishwasher, giving her a chance to answer. When she didn't, he hurried on. "The youth group kids are great. I've chaperoned several of their trips, and they've been a lot of fun."

He didn't know why he was selling the plan so hard. Chaperoning a youth group trip wasn't one of his favorite things, but the youth director was always begging for volunteers, and Matthew helped whenever he was available.

"I don't know," she said, finally.

"It'll be an adventure."

She lifted an eyebrow. "Don't you think the whole dumped-at-the-altar thing is enough of an adventure for one weekend?"

"She's right, Matthew," her mother said as she scooped leftovers into plastic containers. "She has too much on her plate right now to be chasing off in a car with teenagers. Caroline might like to go though."

"Me working with teenagers?" Caroline shook her head. "That's not going to happen."

Matthew turned back to Haley. "I just thought you would like to forget about the wedding business for a few hours."

Haley had already opened her mouth, probably to decline, but she closed it again, appearing to reconsider. "You know, maybe I will go with you. I could use a break from my life."

Trina Scott turned and rested her hip against the counter. "Now Haley, are you sure you want to do that?"

"It will be better than sitting at home feeling sorry for myself. Besides, it will give Elizabeth and me the chance to get to know each other better." She patted the child's head, and Elizabeth grinned up at her.

"She won't be there." Matthew had spoken too quickly, and from the women's expressions, he could tell he wasn't the only one who'd noticed. Just because he didn't want his daughter to spend too much time with Haley didn't mean he needed to be unkind. "I mean…younger kids aren't included in this event. Elizabeth will be spending the night here."

"Oh. It'll be fun anyway, I guess."

Haley appeared disappointed, and Matthew didn't know what to think about that.

"Daddy, I want to go, too," Elizabeth whined. "Why can't I go with Miss Haley? It's not fair."

Matthew sighed inside, preparing himself for his daughter's meltdown. This was a new stage for her, one he was determined to put to an end quickly. But just as he started toward Elizabeth, Haley lifted her up on her hip.

"You get to spend the whole night here with Grammy? You're going to have so much fun."

"That's right. You'll have a blast," he agreed.

Matthew didn't have to look to know his mother was watching him again, sending him another one of those knowing looks. Just because Haley had averted one tantrum didn't mean she was qualified to care for his child. She was still Haley Scott—and all that implied—and he was still Elizabeth's father.

Those truths didn't stop him from feeling badly for Haley though. She'd been through a lot today, and the coming weeks were sure to be difficult.

Maybe it was a bad idea for him to invite her to join him in chaperoning, but he would never be so cruel as to withdraw the invitation.

That didn't keep him from wanting the whole event to just be over with. Then he would have completed his good deed for the day by helping out a woman he'd known since childhood get through a couple of rough days. After that, he could wish her well, and he and Elizabeth could get on with their lives.

Chapter Three

Haley stepped back from the front door, gesturing for Matthew to come inside. She felt strange inviting him in like a guest when he'd visited her mother's new house more times than she had. In fact, everything felt peculiar about her going on this outing with Matthew now, though it had sounded like a good idea last night.

Already she'd spent the morning hanging her incredible wedding gown on the consignment rack at the bridal store and arranging storage for her possessions back in Michigan. Next, she'd "enjoyed" an afternoon of writing thank-you notes for gifts she had to return. Now the idea of accepting an invitation—probably given out of pity—felt like one dose of mortification too many.

Oblivious to her humiliation and appearing fidgety himself, Matthew scanned the room, now stacked with wrapped gifts on one wall and about a dozen packages addressed for return on the opposite wall.

He cleared his throat and turned back to her. "Wow, look at this place. You've been busy."

"Probably too busy. Maybe Mom was right. I am tired. Maybe I should just—"

"Not so fast, Haley Scott."

Haley had been staring at the gifts again, feeling the weight of the work ahead, but she turned to look at him. "Excuse me?"

"You don't know how hard it is to get volunteers for youth group events. Now that you're on the hook, there's no way I'm letting you off."

She snapped her fingers, grimacing. "I knew it. I knew you were only asking me because I was vulnerable and you were short of volunteers."

"Smart gal. Now get your coat. A rowdy bunch of teens are waiting for us."

Forgetting her flimsy argument, Haley did as she was told. Matthew seemed too determined to treat her as his charity case for her to change his mind anyway. For a few seconds last night, she'd wondered if her mother had discouraged her from accepting Matthew's invitation just to trick her into going, but one look at that disapproving frown had ruled out any suspicion of matchmaking motives.

Even the two matchmakers probably recognized the unfortunate timing, and besides, they'd always intended Caroline for Matthew in their silly plan. Not her.

After she retrieved her purse from the bedroom, Haley found Matthew bent in front of the pile of small appliances and stoneware place settings stacked along the wall.

"You've got quite a stash here," he said.

"Two toasters, three waffle irons, a blender and a smoothie maker, and that's without unwrapping any of the ones I hadn't already opened."

"Caroline was right. You should get to keep the loot."

"I don't think so." She shook her head to reinforce her words. "I do wish I could use a form letter for my thank-you notes though. My hand is killing me."

As she flexed and unflexed her left hand, her gaze stopped on her third finger. Her hand looked so bare now without her engagement ring. That piece of jewelry was safe in a drawer upstairs for when she would return it to Tom. The sound of Matthew clearing his throat brought her attention up from her hand.

"Then you need a break…for the sake of those sore fingers. So shall we?" With a tilt of his head, he indicated the front door.

Haley couldn't help smiling as they went outside and descended the steps toward Matthew's hybrid SUV parked at the curb. He was so kind to distract her from her problems. He opened her door before jogging around to the driver's side.

Once inside, he gave her shoulder a squeeze. "Each day will get a little easier, you know."

"How do you—" Haley began, and then she remembered that he did know from experience what it was like to be the one left behind. Though she'd worried briefly about her mother's motives, she found relief in knowing she didn't have to worry about Matthew's. He was reaching out to her in friendship, just as he'd done all those years ago.

Back then his offer had felt like a nightmare, a pat on the head when she'd hoped to be held in his arms. The same offer now seemed perfect. She didn't want or need anything else from a man right now, but she could really use a friend.

The glare from the fluorescent lights caught Haley's attention, and a newborn's distinctive cry filtered down the aisle, as Haley raced through a discount department store, searching for the backdrop for their final photo. Matthew jogged after her, the two girls and two boys they'd shared a ride with in Matthew's SUV earlier taking up the rear.

"Slow down, will you?" the boy named Preston called after her as he stopped and tried to catch his breath.

"You don't want ours to be the last team to get

back to the church, do you?" Haley slowed long enough to ask over her shoulder.

"No, but he doesn't want to collapse and croak next to the health and beauty department, either," an athletic girl named Katie answered for him.

"Good thing for him Haley's headed for the toy department," Matthew said.

Haley grinned as she hurried to the rear of the store. How Matthew knew where she was going, she wasn't sure, but they must have been thinking on the same frequency because they both stopped right in front of a cage-like container of large plastic balls. Great minds did think alike.

"Here. This is perfect." She indicated the cage with an expansive wave.

"You want us to get in there? It's almost smaller than Matt's car." That came from Jimmy, the group's resident comedian.

Haley shook her head. "I just thought we could balance some balls while we build the pyramid."

"Are we going to balance *on* the balls?" Jimmy tried again.

"I don't think so," Matthew said. "We'll really come in last if we have to make a side trip to the E.R. at Markston General."

His deadpan had Haley chuckling. He'd been serious most of the night, through their assignment of squeezing themselves on the store's mini-carousel and her mid-push-up collapse as they did calisthenics on the courthouse steps.

He'd been as serious tonight as he'd been when Haley had seen him with Elizabeth. For someone so blessed with a great career in law and with the opportunity to parent a sweet little girl, Matthew didn't seem to have much fun in his life.

"I wish we could have brought Elizabeth tonight," Haley told him as they waited for Preston to catch up with the group. "She would have loved this."

"It was just for the older kids. Besides, I wouldn't want her to stay up past her bedtime."

Haley nodded, wondering about the strict schedule Matthew and his daughter must keep. Did the house collapse around them if the child went to bed at 8:05 p.m. instead of the top of the hour?

"What are we doing?" Preston asked when he reached them.

"We're deciding how we're going to build the pyramid," Jimmy told him. "We're making you the flier."

Preston shook his head. "Not going to happen."

Matthew raised both hands to garner their attention. "Are we going to build this thing or just talk about it?" When no one answered, he started barking orders. "Three across the bottom. The guys and me. Haley goes with Katie next. Then one on top. Chelsea, that's you."

Each of them grabbed a ball from the bin and settled it between his hands, a chore that became more difficult at each level. After the pyramid was complete, and a little shaky, they looked up to pose for the camera, finding the Polaroid resting forgotten on the floor.

"Wait. Who's going to take the picture?" Jimmy asked.

"Yes. Who's going to take it?"

Haley swallowed as she turned her head in the direction of that unfamiliar voice. A middle-aged woman with a badge that read "Toy Department Manager" stood before them, and she looked anything but pleased.

It took some fast-talking and a promise to leave the store immediately, but they had the picture in their collection when they returned to the vehicle.

As Matthew drove them back to the church, Haley listened to the teens' happy chatter from the second and third rows of seats in the SUV. She might not have been able to agree with their opinions that their photos competed with the work of Ansel Adams, but she had to admit that the outing had been fun.

Maybe Matthew was right. Maybe each day would get a little easier. She just needed to take control of her life and figure out what she would do next. Tonight had only been a night of distraction, but it was a beginning. She would find a way to get on with her life. All she had to do was get through tomorrow—the day she had planned to walk down the aisle.

Matthew held Elizabeth's hand as he walked her from her Sunday school class to the sanctuary where she would sit with his mother while he led the morning music. They'd barely made it into the vestibule, though, before she broke free from him, her black-patent Mary Janes clicking across the tile as she then disappeared into the jungle of adults.

"Elizabeth Ann Warren. Come back here this instant."

He used a louder-than-normal voice, but he shouldn't have bothered. He would never be heard above the din of the Sunday chatter. Checking his watch to make sure he still had a few minutes before the organist would begin the processional, he hurried in the direction she'd taken.

Emerging on the other side of the crowd, he found the group his daughter must have seen first from her waist-high point of view. His mother was talking to Trina Scott, who must have said something clever because all three Scott sisters were laughing. He didn't see a lot to laugh about because his disobedient child was giggling along with them to a punch line she probably didn't understand, and she was doing it from her perch on Haley Scott's hip.

Matthew pinched the bridge of his nose, feeling a headache threatening. Of all those people standing there together, his daughter had to choose Haley to cling to, as if it had been years since she'd seen her instead of days.

"Looking for something?" Haley asked when he strode toward them. She gave the miniature misbehaver in her arms a squeeze, causing the crinolines in the child's dress to crunch. Elizabeth pressed her cheek against Haley's.

Crossing his arms over his chest, Matthew addressed only his daughter. "Young lady, you know better than to run in church. And it's dangerous to run off like that."

"I'm sorry." Elizabeth bent her head and looked up at him from under her eyelashes. "But Miss Haley was here."

As if that explained everything. "Well, I don't want you to do that again, okay?"

"Okay, Daddy."

"Elizabeth was just telling me about her Sunday school lesson." Haley lowered Elizabeth to the floor before straightening the pink-striped blouse she wore with a black skirt. "I love the Noah's ark story, too."

"Animals go two by two," Elizabeth said in a singsongy voice.

His mother touched his shoulder. "Shouldn't you be getting inside?"

Matthew glanced toward the open doors of the sanctuary and then at his watch. The first strains of the organ processional music filtered out the door. He was late. He hated having to go in after the music had already started.

Peeking at his watch once more, he turned back to Elizabeth. "Now I want you to behave for Grammy in church."

The little girl frowned. "I want to sit with Miss Haley."

He opened his mouth to argue, but his mother waved a hand to stop him. "We're all planning to sit together."

"Oh. Good."

Matthew hesitated only a second before waving and making his way to the front of the church. Why was he acting like a protective papa bear this morning, anyway? Everything was under control, just the way he liked it. He'd even hired a perfect, new caregiver for Elizabeth. A pre-med student, who planned to specialize in pediatrics, Renee even came with references.

From his observation point stage left of the pulpit, he watched the two families file in the sanctuary, filling most of the fourth pew. Sure enough, Elizabeth managed to sit next to Haley, but his mother sat on her other side. No big deal.

What harm was it for Elizabeth to befriend Haley anyway? Haley needed friends, apparently better ones than he was being.

He glanced over to his daughter in time to see her pull out a hymnal and hand it to Haley. In the Bible, God had instructed fathers to teach their children in the ways of faith and yet at only four years old, Elizabeth was a better example than Matthew was of how to reach out to others.

Out of the corner of his eye, he caught the organist motioning for him to take his place behind the lectern to lead the opening hymn. Obviously, he needed to listen better to the lessons in church instead of just leading the music.

He did his best to pay close attention to all the morning's hymns and then through Reverend Boggs's sermon on the "Parable of the Lost Sheep." Church sometimes felt like just another obligation, but this time he vowed to search for deeper meanings that he could apply to his life.

Only a few times did he give in to the temptation to glance down at his family, but that was just to make sure his daughter behaved during services. Once he caught Haley holding her index finger to her lips to hush her, but other than that, Elizabeth was a model citizen.

Matthew was proud of Elizabeth's behavior. When Elizabeth and his mother reached him in the receiving line after services, he tried not to notice that she stood there calmly holding Haley's hand when she'd run away from him earlier.

"Well, sweetie, you sure were a well-behaved young lady during church services. Miss Renee will be very happy if you're this good for her tomorrow."

"Daddy, why can't Miss Haley be my new babysitter?"

Matthew stiffened, trying not to look at Haley. "You know why, honey. We hired Miss Renee, and she starts tomorrow."

"I don't want Miss Renee. I want Miss Haley."

"You know Miss Haley will be too busy taking care of the details from the…er…wedding to…" He let the words trail away, not sure what else to say.

"Your daddy's right about that," Haley said.

This time Matthew couldn't help stealing a look at Haley. She was still smiling as she had been when they'd approached, but the look didn't quite reach her eyes.

She bent to get on Elizabeth's level. "Don't worry. I'm sure she'll be nice."

When Haley stood again, her gaze connected with Matthew's. Her sad expression made it clear that she understood his real reason for never even approaching her about the job. She seemed to recognize what he really thought about her, and his opinion hurt.

Something tightened inside his chest. He'd always known that parenting was a tough job.

He'd found that out the hard way when Stacey had left. But he'd never realized that doing what he'd considered to be the right thing for his child—what he *still* thought was the right thing— would make him feel like such a heel.

Chapter Four

Matthew flipped through the stack of papers on his desk for the third time, hoping he'd simply overlooked something, but the legal brief still wasn't there. Not just any legal brief but the one he was supposed to file in court in about, he paused to look at his watch, forty-five minutes. Shoving back his executive chair from his desk, he crossed to the row of filing cabinets on the south wall and yanked open a drawer.

"It has to be here somewhere," he hissed. At least it had better be if he didn't plan to get the chewing out of a lifetime from Judge Andrews for wasting the court's time.

A tap at his office door brought his head around. "Sybil, I told you no visitors," he began. His words fell away, though, when not his office assistant but his daughter and her brand-new child-care provider stepped inside.

"Hi, Daddy." Elizabeth ran inside, scrambling into his office chair.

He didn't have time for this. He didn't even have time for a restroom break, let alone visitors. "Hey, you two," he said, trying to sound calm. "I didn't expect you to come by. Feel free to look around, Renee, but unfortunately, I can't give you the full tour. I'm due in court in a little more than a half hour and I'm missing—"

"That's a bummer," the nineteen-year-old said to interrupt him. "I know you're busy, so I won't keep you long. I wanted to let you know I've found another job, so I won't be able to keep Elizabeth after all."

"So you've come to give notice?" So much for the future pediatrician being the perfect sitter.

"I would. Really. Sorry." She at least had the decency to look guilty. "But they needed someone right away. Today even. I'll be working as a receptionist at a posh health club. I can study any time I'm not answering a call, and it pays better money than—" She stopped herself but not before she'd made her point.

Matthew shoved his hands in his pockets to keep from fisting them. "You can't be serious."

"I said I'm sorry it didn't work out. Elizabeth's been bawling all morning, anyway, and asking for someone named Haley. I would never get any studying done with all of that racket."

As if that made what she'd just done to him okay. Before he could argue further, Renee waved and backed out of the door, leaving him alone with his child, who climbed down and crawled under his desk. He'd never been able to tempt Elizabeth with the box of toys he kept in one of his office cabinets when his big office desk served as the best clubhouse for a four-year-old.

Matthew started ticking off a list of possible sitters on his fingers. His mother? No, she and Mrs. Scott were meeting with his mom's accountant this morning. Dylan? Matthew shook his head. His brother had already complained about his heavy patient load today.

Not that he liked to rely on Logan…but Logan? Grabbing his phone, he dialed his brother's number at the park ranger's office, but when the machine answered, he slammed the phone back into its cradle. He ground his teeth, probably ruining years of good dental care. What was he supposed to do now?

An idea slid, unwelcome, into his thoughts, and he would have dismissed it out of hand, but he had neither the time nor the luxury. He knew one person who'd already proven she was great with kids, and his own child just happened to love her. For right now, that had to be enough. Resigned, he lifted the handset and dialed again.

"Hey, Haley," he said when she answered on the second ring.

"Matthew, is that you? Is something wrong?"

Guilt twisted inside him. Even Haley recognized that he wouldn't call her unless he needed something. "As a matter of fact, I am in a bind."

"What is it?"

Matthew took a deep breath and then filled her in on the details. He spoke quickly because it was going to take some convincing to get past the fact that he'd offended her yesterday.

He finished with "I know you're probably busy, but if you could possibly help me out…" Letting his words trail away, he braced himself for a chewing out more acidic than even Judge Andrews would be giving him in—another glance at the watch—twenty-nine minutes.

On the other end of the line, Haley cleared her throat. "I'll be there in ten minutes."

She didn't say more, only clicked off the phone. Matthew let out the breath he'd been holding. He didn't have to ask himself who'd been the bigger person today. That answer was clear in the grinning face of the little girl who crawled out from beneath his desk.

"Is Miss Haley going to be my babysitter?"

As frustrated as he was with his daughter's behavior, he could only put out one fire at a time, and his eyebrows were already singed enough from the one he'd just extinguished. Anyway, if he didn't find that brief in the next twenty-four minutes, he would have humiliated himself by asking for Haley's help for nothing.

"Just for today. Play there for a few minutes while we wait for her."

He didn't have to tell her twice. She disappeared beneath the desk again.

Hurrying back to the filing cabinet, Matthew threw open a drawer. Since he'd already searched the Lively file on his desk, he didn't know where to begin looking for the misfiled document.

"Daddy."

"Just a minute, honey. I'm busy."

"But Daddy—"

His jaw flexing, he shot an annoyed glance toward his desk. Elizabeth stood just in front of the chair holding a messy stack of papers. His documents that had somehow fallen under the desk.

"It's dirty under there."

"It certainly is. Thank you for picking it up."

Now he had two people to thank for cleaning up his mess and one of them was too young to understand the importance of what she'd found. He'd put the documents in order and was tucking them in his briefcase when Haley rushed through the door, her winter coat flapping open.

She brushed her hand back through her hair

that was messier than normal and then glanced down at her sport pants and sweatshirt and the athletic shoes she wore without socks. "I wasn't expecting to go out today."

"I'm glad you did. Hey, thanks—"

"No problem," she said to interrupt him. "Now where's that Elizabeth hiding?" Though she asked the question, she walked right toward the desk where the child was hiding again.

Elizabeth popped out, pushing back the office chair. "I'm here." She scrambled over to Haley and hugged her around the waist.

"Hey, you. We're going to have tons of fun today, aren't we?" Hefting Elizabeth on her hip, she turned back to Matthew. "Shouldn't you be going?"

He glanced at the door and then at his watch. Fifteen minutes. "Judge Andrews doesn't look favorably on tardiness."

"Then go ahead." She snuggled Elizabeth to her shoulder. "We'll be fine."

Matthew gave Haley his address, handed her the house key and then grabbed his coat and briefcase. They would be fine; he knew that. And he would do what he had to do. He had to push aside any misgivings and get on with it. Still, like so many times in a parent's life, he could only hope he'd made the right decision.

"Daddy's home!"

The sound of the garage-door opener confirmed

Elizabeth's announcement as she dropped her doll in the middle of her miniature fashion show. She raced from the living room, through the kitchen, to the door that separated the house from the garage.

Haley set her doll aside to place all the dresses and tiny pumps of every color in Elizabeth's toy suitcase.

From the other room, she could hear the sweet exchange that was probably the daily ritual in the Warren house.

"Hi, Daddy."

"Hey, munchkin. Did you have a good day?"

At the sound of the door closing and footsteps coming from the kitchen, Haley stiffened. It didn't seem right for her to be so nervous now, not after she and Elizabeth had just spent such a wonderful afternoon together, but she couldn't help hoping Matthew would be impressed by her efforts. The events of the last few days must have really done a number on her if she was this desperate for an *attaboy*.

Matthew and his daughter came through the doorway hand in hand. Haley waved at them from the floor.

"Hello." He glanced her way but then started scanning the room.

Haley followed the path of his gaze, at first wondering what he was looking for and then annoyed by her guess. Did he expect to find structural damage in his home or something? Wasn't it enough that he'd asked her to care for Elizabeth only after he'd probably exhausted other possibilities? He seemed determined to offend her today.

"It was so fun." Elizabeth moved to stay in front of her father's sliding gaze. "We played toys and read books and ate peanut butter and watched cartoons and—"

"That's nice, honey," he said to interrupt her since she wasn't likely to stop listing every detail.

He must have found no bullet holes or burn marks on the wall because Matthew finally turned back to Haley. "Thank you for doing this."

"A whole day and not a single emergency room visit. A real feat," she couldn't resist commenting.

When he looked back at her, he wore a guilty expression. Well, he deserved to feel guilty. If he thought she would be such a bad influence on his child, then he shouldn't have asked her at all.

"Elizabeth seemed to have a good day."

"Does that surprise you?"

Matthew blinked, her question startling him more than any observation. With her innocent question, Haley asked about far more than his thoughts on how his daughter spent her day. She had every right to ask him what his problem was, too, but he didn't have an answer for her. At least not a good one.

Unlike Renee, who'd dumped his child with him as soon as a better offer came along, Haley had dropped everything to help him. She'd given up her whole day to care for Elizabeth and even left the house passably neat. She'd done all that, and all he could manage was a banal thank-you. The least he could do was to be more grateful. A little humility couldn't hurt, either.

He cleared his throat. "No, that doesn't surprise me. Elizabeth thinks you're great."

Haley was putting away the last of the dolls, but she stopped and looked at him, lifting a brow. Her assumption that Elizabeth's father didn't think she was all that great couldn't have been clearer.

"I want you to know how much I appreciate you stepping in for us today. We were really in a pinch."

"I did it for Elizabeth."

Until then, Elizabeth hadn't appeared to be paying attention to the conversation, but she looked up and announced, "Miss Haley did it for me."

The words Haley had spoken and Elizabeth reinforced rang as true in his ears as any statement a credible witness made during cross-examination. Haley had stepped forward for the child's sake even though she understood she wasn't the candidate he would have chosen. Wasn't that similar to what he tried to do with Elizabeth, always putting her needs ahead of anything else?

"Well, thanks." His throat felt tight as he looked from Haley to Elizabeth. He reached down and tugged one of his daughter's braids. "How about we put in a video for you while Miss Haley and I talk?"

"Okay."

He led Elizabeth into the family room and inserted an old video that he'd only recently come to hate because she watched it so often. When he returned to the living room, he gestured for Haley to follow him into the kitchen. He took a seat at the table.

"Here, come sit with me."

Haley chewed her bottom lip, but she took the seat opposite his. She fidgeted with a ring on her left pinkie, slipping it on and off several times. Finally, she looked up at him.

"What did you want to talk about?" She brushed at a piece of fuzz on her sweatshirt.

"A job," he blurted before he could think better of it. "I know you gave up yours when you left Michigan."

"I know." She stared at her hands twisting her ring around. "There's nothing left for me in Muskegon. Even Jenna lives on the other side of

Michigan. I need to start looking for a new job, but I haven't even decided where I'm going to live. Mom said I could stay with her until I figure things out, but I don't know if that's a good idea."

"You don't have to decide right away."

Her head came up then. "This coming from Matthew Warren, the king of advanced-planning-for-the-future? The expert of dotted *I*s and crossed *T*s."

He shook his index finger at her. "Could we wait until later to denigrate my character? I'm trying to make you an offer here."

"I probably could wait until seven thirty," she began, but stopped in the middle of her joke. She tilted her head and studied him. "Offer? You mean a job offer?"

His hands went up in a reflexive move. "Just a temporary one. I would like you to watch Elizabeth until I find a suitable child-care provider."

Smiling, Matthew waited for her reaction. And waited. Her bland expression offered no hints about what she was thinking.

"How could I resist an offer like that?" she said finally.

It wasn't the enthusiastic reaction he'd expected, given how taken Haley seemed to be with Elizabeth, but he pressed on anyway, so his own misgivings wouldn't get the best of him. "So you'll do it?"

She nodded.

"Oh, good. So do you think you could commit to the job for, oh, let's say, one month?" Something seemed to cloud the blue sky of her eyes, but Matthew tried not to read anything into it. "I can even draft a contract to that effect. Then we'll both know we're on the same page."

Haley pushed back from the table, stood and crossed to the sink without looking at him. Turning on the faucet, she took out a glass, then filled it and took a sip. He'd offended her just as he had at church the day before. At first the contract had seemed like a good idea, even necessary given Haley's work history, but now it felt mean.

He was already out of his chair and approaching from behind her to apologize when Haley turned to face him.

"I need you to know," she paused as if weighing her words, "that what I said to you earlier was the truth but maybe not the whole truth. I did step in today for Elizabeth's sake, but I also did it for you."

"I know that." And because he did know it, he also recognized that one of them had grown up to be a nicer person than the other. "I'm sorry for suggesting the contract."

"It's fine. I'll even sign one if it will make you more comfortable."

He shook his head. "That won't be necessary."

"Okay, then." She poured out the water and put the glass in the dishwasher.

"So we're agreed on one month?" Maybe he was willing to forego the contract, but he was a lawyer after all, and he needed to come to some sort of official agreement.

When Haley glanced over her shoulder at him, her smile suggested that she understood his need to have all the details at least signed on the imaginary line.

"There's one more thing you should know. I'm here for Elizabeth *and you,* and I'll be here for as long as you need me."

Chapter Five

Haley couldn't help grinning at the disaster zone of her mother's usually spotless living room. Opened boxes of stoneware and flatware place settings virtually buried the coffee table, and pastel ribbons and gift wrap littered the floor. Her sisters were sprawled in the middle of the chaos, cheering on Elizabeth who gleefully tossed handfuls of bows into the air.

"We should invite Mrs. Warren over," Haley suggested. "She would really appreciate this place. It looks just like an exploding wedding cake."

"You'll be picking up every single paper and ribbon scrap of this *explosion,* young lady," Trina Scott said from her chair where she'd been viewing with disapproval the activities of the last half hour.

"Don't say things like that, Mom. You just gave me a scary childhood flashback."

"Haley Lynne Scott…"

At the warning in her mother's voice, Haley popped up from the spot where she'd been sitting cross-legged on the floor and bent to kiss her mother's dark hair. "Ah, come on, Mom. We're having fun. Anyway, I doubt my wedding guests would mind if Elizabeth opens a few of the gifts. We're still returning them, aren't we?"

"Of course, we are," Caroline supplied. To emphasize her point, she plopped down a cardboard box that she'd just addressed to one of the wedding guests. "We should have it all done before Jenna and I go home this weekend."

Jenna caught Elizabeth around the waist and stuck a bow to the top of her head. "I don't know about the rest of you, but I was dying to know what was inside those boxes."

"You mean the stuff that Haley only would have been allowed to keep if she'd made the biggest mistake of her life by marrying Tom?" Caroline's words dripped of sarcasm.

At the mention of her ex-fiancé's name, Haley braced herself and waited for the pain to return. A twinge of discomfort filled her, but it was nothing compared to the ache and humiliation she'd felt a few days before. Would it continue that way, hurting a little less each time someone spoke about her wedding?

Trina glanced sidelong at her firstborn as she

leaned forward in her chair. "Okay, we get it, Caroline. You think wedding gifts are passé. Maybe you think that single-gal showers should be the new trend."

"Don't laugh," Caroline said, wrinkling her nose. "A *single-gal shower* as you call it probably will be the only kind you'll ever plan for me because I'll never prance down any aisle."

This wasn't the first time Caroline had mentioned that she never planned to marry, but Trina Scott had always sidestepped that topic. Even now she sent her daughter a look that said, "We'll see about that."

"Oh, did I mention that Amy wanted us to go out with them for pizza tonight?" Trina asked.

"Who's 'them'?" Caroline said with a frown.

"Will Dylan be there?" Jenna asked hopefully.

Trina shook her head. "It's just us and Amy, Matthew and young Elizabeth here." She reached out to brush the child's arm as she scampered past.

Haley chewed her lip, trying not to laugh. Their mother clearly wasn't going to give up this matchmaking thing. She was like a bulldog with a particularly juicy bone: she wasn't about to let it go.

"Stop meddling, Mother," Caroline said.

"I don't know what you're talking about." Trina crossed her arms over her chest and settled back into her chair. "Anyway, I never meddle. I mother."

"We're especially blessed, then." Haley paused, casting a conspiratorial glance at her sisters. "Because you *mother* us better than anybody."

Jenna and Carolina both covered their mouths with their hands to hide their laughter, but Trina quelled it with that same stern look that always had made them straighten up during church services.

"Now that's better." Their mother's voice was pleasant, and a hint of a smile appeared on her lips.

Haley peeked over at Caroline, pitying someone else for the first time all week. Caroline had every reason to be worried as far as Haley was concerned.

Usually when Trina Scott wanted something, there was nothing that could stop her from making it happen. Unless God had other plans, anyway. This time Trina appeared to want Matthew Warren for a son-in-law, so Caroline had better watch out or she'd be picking a china pattern before she could make her happy-to-be-single speech again.

Even with Caroline's determination, Haley couldn't blame her mother for giving her match-making a try with those two. Probably no one in North America had more in common with

Caroline than Matthew had. Classic overachieving firstborns, both filtered intensity and drive through their pores the way other people sweated frustration.

Pairing them would be one for the record books. Just the thought of it made Haley smile but no more than her incredulity that she'd once imagined herself as a good match for Matthew Warren did. And roommates Felix and Oscar of the old TV show *The Odd Couple* thought they'd had it bad.

Caroline must have caught sight of Haley's grin because she narrowed her gaze.

Elizabeth saved Haley from having to answer that unspoken question by crouching in front of her. "Can I open another present, Miss Haley? Just one more. Please?" Already, she had the paper off a box that contained a dessert service set.

"You absolutely *may,* little Lizzie." Haley reached for a wad of gift wrap and tossed it in a trash bag. "Just make sure you put the cards with the presents so we know where to return them."

"You'd better watch calling her 'Lizzie,'" her mother warned. "Matthew doesn't like anyone shortening his daughter's name. He doesn't like anyone interfering with his parenting decisions, either. Not even his own mother."

"Ah." Haley waved away the warning with a

brush of her hand. "You worry too much. It's just a name, anyway, and hers is too big for someone so small."

"Don't say I didn't warn you."

Haley winced at her mother's words that sounded all too familiar. From when she'd changed her business major to computer science and then to sociology. From when she'd taken that night job at the animal shelter. From when she'd decided to give up her most recent job before the wedding.

Haley had to admit that some of those times—okay, all of them—her mother had been right. This time just wasn't one of them. Haley had been around Matthew and Elizabeth enough to know that he needed to lighten up with his daughter, and maybe she was just the person to show him how to do it. How could anyone live with so many rules?

Still, she would take her mother's warning seriously about Matthew's refusal to take parenting suggestions, and she would try to call his daughter by her given name. If Haley offended him now, he might forget about their one-month agreement and begin searching for her replacement right away. She didn't want that to happen, and not just because she really needed this job, either.

She'd had more fun caring for Elizabeth these

past three days than she'd ever had in any job. Elizabeth was just amazing. Clever and creative and funny. It just so happened that Elizabeth needed Haley to care for her, and Haley liked the idea of being needed.

Did Matthew even realize the blessing he'd been given to parent this sweet girl? Haley was just getting to know her, and already she knew. She couldn't get enough of seeing the child's inviting smile or hearing her innocent observations of the world.

Yes, Elizabeth needed more fun and less structure in her life, but letting Matthew know that Haley thought so right away might be a mistake. She'd already told him she would be there for him and his daughter for as long as they needed her, and she intended to keep her word, especially since they seemed to need her more than she'd thought. As long as Matthew would allow her to, she would give Elizabeth some of the fun that was clearly missing from her life.

Matthew held his breath late that afternoon as he drove down his lane. Not that he was worried that Haley wouldn't keep Elizabeth safe while he wasn't home. His instincts told him to trust her there. But beyond that given, he didn't know what to expect when he pulled up to the house.

Just yesterday he'd found a mammoth,

rainbow-colored chalk mural covering his driveway and two laughing "artists" trying to scrub chalk dust off their clothes in the laundry room. He couldn't blame them for wanting to get outside on one of those summer-teaser days that Indiana experienced every winter, but did his daughter really have to miss her nap to work on her graffiti masterpiece?

As if throwing off Elizabeth's schedule wasn't enough, Haley hadn't even bothered to hose off the cement, just leaving it there and waiting for rain…or snow.

The quiet struck him as soon as he pulled into the garage and cut the engine. Where the rumble of tiny running feet should have reverberated from inside the house, there was silence. Come to think of it, Matthew couldn't remember seeing Haley's silver two-door car parked on the street.

He unlocked the garage entry and stepped into the kitchen, finding it empty as he'd predicted. No dishes were piled in the sink, and not a single game littered the floor. From the looks of it, they'd been gone all day.

Matthew rubbed his temples. Yes, a headache was definitely coming on. Wasn't it enough that he had to make a command appearance tonight at another Warren-Scott get-together? Especially when he would spend the whole night dodging attempts by his mother and Mrs. Scott to shove him and Caroline together. Now he would probably have to deal with a grouchy child, as well, because Elizabeth had missed her nap while she and Haley were gallivanting.

As Matthew flipped open his cell phone, the sound of an engine filtered through the open garage door. He popped his head outside the kitchen door just as Elizabeth's pink and white sneakers came pounding across the cement. He stepped into the garage to meet her.

"You beat us home, Daddy."

"I guess I did. So, where've you been?"

"We played all day at Mrs. Scott's house." Elizabeth announced it like she'd just received a cavity-free report at the dentist.

"What about your nap?"

"I wasn't sleepy," she said with a triumphant smile.

"I see."

He turned his attention toward the driveway and the approach of the woman responsible for all the whining he'd heard last night and would again tonight. He had no one to blame but himself for hiring someone with Haley's track record to fill in as his child-care provider. How could he expect her to understand the importance of schedules and structure in a child's life when she had neither of those things in her own?

Haley looked back at him guiltily. "We got

caught up addressing the packages and lost track of time. You know…the wedding gifts."

She must have thrown in the last comment as some flimsy form of protection from his censure. To his shame, it worked. At least it kept him from coming down on her like a piano on a broken pulley lift. Maybe he should give her a break. Not yet a week since she'd been dumped, she still had a truckload of wedding gifts to return.

"I opened all the presents for Miss Haley," Elizabeth said importantly.

"Yes. Lizzie was a big help."

Matthew stiffened. "Her name is Elizabeth. I would appreciate your calling her that."

"Oh. Sorry. Elizabeth I mean."

His daughter looked up, surprised, but then she shot back to the car. She riffled around in the backseat and returned with a necklace made of string and dozens of bows.

"Look at what Miss Haley gave me."

"That was nice of her, but…" He let his words trail off because Elizabeth wasn't paying attention to him. She was too busy modeling the necklace for her audience of two.

Matthew nodded his approval before turning back to Haley. "I assume you've heard about the plans for tonight."

"Pizza with Grammy!" Elizabeth jumped as

she said it, her necklace lifting and falling with each bounce.

"Yeah, pizza. We're all over that." Haley crossed over and gave Elizabeth a high-five.

"I just hope Elizabeth won't be too tired to enjoy it. She really does need her nap."

"I'm sorry."

"Nothing we can do about it now. But from now on, I would like Elizabeth to be home in her bed for at least one hour of rest time each afternoon."

"Absolutely. Come on, Elizabeth. Let's get you cleaned up and ready to go out to dinner."

As he watched the exchange, Matthew felt a jolt of adrenaline like those he experienced in the courtroom when the judge ruled on his side. He'd won on this point at least. But when Haley started bunny hopping toward the house, and Elizabeth joined in behind her, holding her hands on her sitter's hips, Matthew felt the way he did when a case went awry.

Elizabeth was crazy about Haley. The disciplined dad versus the festive friend—he was sure to come up short. Reason told him he didn't have to compete: he was the only father Elizabeth had. Still, he had to tamp back his insecurities.

He couldn't allow himself to worry about competing. This was parenting, not a popularity contest. His job never came with the promise of balloons and confetti. He alone held the responsibility for molding a young life. He couldn't afford to fall short on that duty by giving Haley free reign over his daughter.

After this evening's festivities, he would have a discussion with Haley. He would lay down the rules for the Warren household, and she would have to get on board or he would— He stopped himself. What exactly would he do? Fire Haley and cart Elizabeth to court with him every day? Perhaps he could send Elizabeth to Amy's Elite Treats with his mother like a store pet. Or he could pack her off to Dylan's optometry office or, worse yet, the state park with Ranger Logan.

There was no perfect solution here and certainly none that would provide even the minimal stability he wanted for his child: that of being in her own house. Except one.

He blew out a frustrated breath. No, Haley was not the perfect sitter. Not even close. She believed beds could be made any time of the day and it was okay to watch cartoons before breakfast. Even imperfect, Haley was still the best solution he had for the time being. And she might even do a passable job with some strict guidance.

Matthew rubbed his forehead, a full-blown headache now thrumming beneath his fingertips. Even thinking of it as a temporary solution wasn't enough to soothe his worries. Elizabeth was already becoming more attached to Haley than he would like.

He could only imagine what a few more weeks would do to that situation. Was he setting up his daughter for more pain by allowing her to form a deep connection with another woman who would soon disappear from her life? He'd had no control when his wife had left, but now he would have no one to blame but himself.

The situation felt like a pending court date when his case wasn't even close to being prepared. No matter what Haley had said about being there for as long as his family needed her and how dedicated she appeared to be right now, she was bound to lose interest and find a new project soon.

So it would be in everyone's best interests if he acted fast to find a permanent replacement. This would give him the chance to thank Haley for the help and send her on her merry way before her attention span reached its breaking point. Perhaps it would even spare his child from dealing with a broken heart.

Chapter Six

Just after the dinner rush, four Scotts and three Warrens squeezed into the largest booth at the downtown pizza eatery called The Pie. Haley would have suggested that they'd be more comfortable at one of those long tables in the back of the room if the two mothers didn't appear downright giddy with the arrangement. Mrs. Warren had picked out the table herself, telling the waiter it looked cozy. Then they engineered it so that Matthew and Caroline were sitting next to each other. Could they be more obvious?

Even with rolling her eyes, and her elbows imprinting her sides and her knees bumping Jenna's every time she shifted, Haley couldn't help but notice the restaurant's charm. Warmth radiated through the open dining room as flames flickered inside yellow globes and old friends gathered around tables covered with checked vinyl cloths.

Somehow, though, she doubted that Matthew and Caroline were enjoying the atmosphere as much, not with their mothers looking at them with so much expectation. Such hope. Even now Haley's mother was watching Matthew over the top of her menu, her reading glasses perched on her nose. "What do you like on your pizza, Matthew?"

"I don't know." Matthew didn't look up from where he was reading menu options. "I'll eat pretty much anything on it. Except anchovies."

Trina's face lit up like a child's at a birthday party. "Well, isn't that a coincidence? Caroline likes her pizza loaded, too. She's the only one in the family. Her sisters won't eat anything but cheese on theirs."

"That is a coincidence," Matthew said dryly, his gaze still squarely on the menu.

"I like anchovies," Caroline was quick to point out.

"And you admit that in public?" Jenna's eyebrow was so high that it disappeared behind her light brown bangs.

Haley pressed her lips together to keep from laughing. All this time, she'd been looking for a complicated compatibility formula for dating when according to the meddling matriarchs here, the answers to the human heart could be found in a steaming slice of pizza.

No. Wait. She and Tom were both flavor purists, insisting that adding anything to the trio tastes of sauce, mozzarella and crust was just overkill. So she could tell her mother and Mrs. Warren right now that pizza compatibility wasn't the secret.

Pushing aside the thought, Haley focused on poor Caroline and Matthew, who were sandwiched so tightly together that their knees had to be bumping. If they felt half as uncomfortable as Matthew had made her feel when he'd arrived home from work today, then she pitied them. She wouldn't wish that on anyone.

As if she needed another reminder of that face-off with Matthew, Haley peeked at the child seated next to her father. The usually vivacious little girl sat with her elbows planted on the table, a surly expression on her face. Already, she'd whined in Matthew's car all the way to the restaurant, and her attitude didn't appear on the upswing.

A waiter sporting a T-shirt with the words "Eat a Pie" approached then, carrying a large bowl of tossed salad and a stack of plates.

Amy Warren gave the order for two large pizzas—one loaded and one cheese-only—before taking her granddaughter's hand on one side and her best friend's on the other. When all their hands were linked, she bowed her head and began to pray.

"Father God, thank You for this opportunity to spend time with our dear friends. Please bless this food and guide us as we seek to build deeper connections between our families for the future. In Your Son's name, Amen."

As they released hands, Amy reached for the salad bowl and tongs as if she hadn't just prayed for a blessing on their matchmaking scheme. Haley wouldn't have been surprised if she prayed next for the quick arrival of their pizza order.

"They have the best salad here," Trina said as her friend passed her the bowl.

Again, Haley had the urge to laugh, but she changed the subject instead. "Now where did you say the other guys were tonight?"

"You mean besides finding any excuse possible not to be here?" Matthew chimed, earning a severe enough frown from his mother to make Haley sit straighter in her seat.

"You know perfectly well that Dylan is catching up on paperwork at the office after his conference, and Logan had to help a friend move into her new apartment."

"Did you say 'her'?" He looked at her over the frames of his glasses, and then he lifted a shoulder and lowered it. "As I said…any excuse."

"I hope we don't miss seeing them completely," Jenna said to no one in particular as she held a pizza slice suspended in front of her mouth. "Caroline and I fly out on Sunday."

"Oh, can't you stay longer?" Amy asked.

Though it couldn't have been clearer that she was interested in extending the stay of just one of the Scott sisters, Caroline answered for them both. "Not if we plan to keep our jobs."

Sunday probably wouldn't be soon enough for Caroline, who'd sworn off relationships only to have her mother turn a deaf ear on her pronouncement. Even though Haley wasn't feeling pressure from good-intentioned meddlers, she could understand the urge to put some space between herself and Matthew Warren.

What she'd ever seen in the guy all those years ago, she had a hard time remembering now. Matthew could give curmudgeon lessons in his spare time. In fact, if it weren't for her promise to watch Elizabeth and the fact that Haley had nowhere else to go, she would have been catching her own jet plane along with her sisters.

Next to Matthew, Elizabeth continued to sit with her elbows planted on the table, her slice of pizza untouched on the plate in front of her.

Matthew cleared his throat and made some sort of signal to her with a tilt of his head. His daughter removed her elbows, but her scowl remained firmly in place. Matthew's jaw tightened, his gaze trained on Haley rather than his child. Elizabeth looked as morose as her father did, and the child's mood was Haley's fault because she hadn't respected Matthew's rules.

Apprehension filled her gut. She could hope for the best, perhaps a shorter than average dinner, but she suspected this night wouldn't end well.

"What kind of books do you like to read, Matthew?"

He turned back to Haley's mother, caught off guard by her remark, especially when he was too busy grumbling at Haley to stay on his toes for the next round in the matchmaking game.

"I don't get to read for pleasure often these days. I read a lot of law books and hymnals, though."

Haley was ready to give him points for a smooth sidestep, but her mother wasn't having any of it. "I didn't ask what you *do* read. I asked what you *like* to read."

Poor guy, he didn't stand a chance. Haley knew perfectly well that Matthew had never been able to resist the classics. Even when they were children, while his brothers were in video-game trances, trying to get to the next tasty level of "Alien Fighter Jelly Beans" or some such, Matthew could always be found on the couch, kicking back with Dickens or Hemingway. The situation had been the same in the Scott household, with Caroline as the reader, except for the "Alien Fighter Jelly Beans" part.

The funny thing was that Mom knew all this perfectly well, too. If she was already counting on a tentative merger between Caroline and Matthew based a common enjoyment of pepperoni and black olives, then she surely expected their shared love of *Beowulf* and *To Kill a Mockingbird* to seal the deal.

"The classics are probably my favorite," he told her.

"Of course. Now I remember." Trina could have earned herself a Tony Award nomination for that over-the-top stage version of surprise. "Did you know that Caroline is a fan of the classics, too?"

"I do remember that," he answered blandly.

Haley hoped her mother wasn't trying to be sly with this interrogation because she was about as subtle as a steamroller taking down a rubber duck. If she really wanted to know something new about Matthew, she could ask him why he hadn't spoken to his child's sitter all night or why he kept tossing sour looks her way. But clearly Trina was on a mission, and that mission didn't involve intervening between Haley and her boss.

"Do you enjoy classical music, as well, because Caroline—"

Haley didn't know whether to be horrified or relieved when Elizabeth interrupted the next round of the sales pitch by letting out a shriek that made the globed oil lamp on their table vibrate.

"I don't want any dumb pizza!"

"Elizabeth."

Matthew's warning voice would have silenced Haley, but Elizabeth must have taken it as encouragement because her voice became a wail.

"No pizza! No pizza!" Bracing both hands on the edge of the table, Elizabeth pushed back her chair, at the end of the booth, sending it teetering backward.

Matthew leaped to his feet, deftly nabbing the back of the chair with one hand and his daughter's pint-size form with the other. His arm slipped around her waist, allowing her limbs to dangle downward. Though Elizabeth wailed, her flailing arms and legs occasionally connecting with his thigh or side, he didn't even look at her.

His glare was for Haley alone.

"Well, we've had about enough fun for one evening." He turned to his mother and her best friend. "Forgive us, but we have to call it a night."

From the hooks adorning the booth, he retrieved coats, shoved them under his free arm and then strode to the door. As Matthew moved aside for the host to open the heavy wooden door for him, Haley watched, waiting for him to glance her way before he crossed through the doorway. They'd come together after all. He didn't look back even once.

As the door swung closed, it appeared to Haley

that more than a man and his overtired child were slipping away through that sliver of remaining light. She couldn't let him leave. Not without at least another apology.

She turned back to the other women watching their exit as she had been. "I'm sorry. I have to go, too."

"But all this pizza." Her mother was frowning, probably more for the loss of Matthew's company than hers.

"Just package it up. I love it cold." Haley put an arm into her coat sleeve. "It reminds me of college."

With that, she hurried across the room and out the door. She was responsible for this outburst, so she owed it to him to help now if she could. She caught up to him outside, just as the parking lot lights switched on. Busy wrestling someone from the thirty-five-pound weight class into the shoulder strap of her car booster seat, he didn't notice Haley's approach.

"Now hold still, silly. Let me get this done so I can get you to bed."

"I don't want bed." Instead of a shriek, this time her words came out with a sniffling moan.

"I know you don't, but you're tired. You'll feel better in the morning."

"I'm not sleepy," she whined.

Finally, Matthew must have had her buckled the way he liked because he closed the back door and pulled open the driver's-side door. His shoulders stiffened the moment he saw Haley standing a few steps away.

"What are you doing out here?"

Haley pulled her coat closed over her neck. "We rode together, remember?"

"I need to get her home." He gestured to the child already dozing and unaffected by the dome light. "I'm sure one of the others will give you a ride home."

"My car's at your house."

"Oh. Right."

Haley could almost see the wheels turning in his mind as he thought of a way to avoid sharing oxygen with her for another minute. And because Markston wasn't so big, he could make the point that his house would not have been out of the way for the others.

Still, his practicality must have won out because he crossed to the passenger side and opened the door for her. He acknowledged her thanks with a nod, but the cold in his eyes trumped even the wind blowing in before he closed it. The music of Bach or Mozart or some other dead guy filtered into the car when he started the engine, but he flipped it off with a click. The kind of silence that would have made a librarian proud settled around them, making the five-minute drive feel like an interstate trek.

Finally, he turned into his driveway and hit the garage-door opener on his visor, but instead of pulling in, he shut off the engine in the driveway. Sensor-activated lights on either side of the two garage doors flicked on, illuminating the car's interior.

As if they'd timed it, both turned back to check on Elizabeth at the same time. She slept heavily now, nothing in her repose hinting that she could feel the chill inside the car. Haley couldn't help smiling when she looked at her. So sweet. Innocent. Completely trusting in a world where real trust was rare.

When Haley finally turned her head and shoulder back toward the front seat, Matthew was staring right at her. Through her was more like it. Haley held her breath. As much as she hated silence, she sensed that what was to follow it this time wouldn't be better.

"Haley, this isn't going to work out."

"What do you mean?" she asked, though she had an inkling.

He exhaled heavily and pressed his lips together before he spoke again. "Your caring for Elizabeth. I don't think this was a good idea."

"No. Wait, Matthew—"

"I knew it, too. I knew it." He seemed to be saying it more to himself than to her. "Why didn't I trust my own instincts?"

"What are you saying?" She shot a glance back at the sleeping child, who'd already created a place for herself in her heart.

Matthew stared into the rearview mirror instead of looking at her. "A child needs structure. How can I expect you to give that when you don't have any of it in your own life? You probably don't know what it is."

"I know what 'structure' is." Even she could hear the crack in her voice, so she didn't try to convince herself that he could have missed it.

Matthew startled and then looked over at her. "Look, I'm sorry. I'm not trying to hurt your feelings here. You're a great girl…um, woman… but…" He let his words fall away, apparently not sure what else to say.

There's always a *but,* isn't there? For the flash of a second, Haley was that fourteen-year-old again, hearing Matthew's kind, if bumbling, attempt to let her down easy after she'd professed her feelings to him. But she couldn't allow herself to go there. Not this time when what he was saying mattered so much more than an unrequited crush.

"I'm really sorry for letting Elizabeth miss her nap."

Already he was shaking his head. "It's not just that. It's…oh, I don't know…everything."

She waited for him to list her infractions, but

he didn't, so she could only guess that there were many. "I know I'm a bit…unconventional—"

"To say the least."

Haley swallowed and tried again. "I can do better. I'll do whatever you need me to. I'll follow your schedule. I'll do it your way. Whatever you want. I need this job." She needed Elizabeth, too. It was probably pitiful to admit it, but she'd never felt more valued than she did by a child who needed her care.

"I'm sorry, Haley. I don't think—"

"But I love her, Matthew."

He had opened his mouth to finish what he'd planned to say, words that would take away the only thing that had made sense to her since she'd moved back to Markston. Now he closed it, darting his tongue out to moisten his lips.

Haley studied him, waiting. Had she said the one thing that would make a difference to Matthew? She wasn't sure, but she took a chance anyway. She couldn't explain why, but it had suddenly become critical to her that she had the opportunity to stay here caring for Elizabeth. She needed that child, and Elizabeth needed her. Whether he realized it or not, Matthew needed her help, too.

"Remember, it's only temporary," she reminded him. "Only until you find a permanent child-care provider. Come on. Give me a second chance."

He shook his head again. "I don't know. It just doesn't seem like a good idea."

"I thought all Christians believed in second chances. Don't you?"

As soon as she said it, Haley realized she'd gone too far. If nothing she'd said before had changed his mind, then calling Matthew's faith into question certainly wasn't going to do it. She stared at his profile and waited for his jaw to tighten the way it always did when he was annoyed. Instead, she was surprised to see the side of his mouth lift.

"Are you sure you want to pose that question to someone who earns at least part of his income filing wrongful death lawsuits? Family members of victims don't get any second chances, and there are those who believe the defendants don't deserve them, either."

Haley shrugged. She had no doubt which group Matthew fell into. There were no shades of gray in Matthew Warren's world, only the blackest black and the whitest white.

That didn't leave her with much of an answer, but because he still seemed to expect one, she remarked, "Should have known better than to argue with an attorney."

"I'll see you at 7:30 a.m. tomorrow."

Haley gave him a sharp glance. "Wait. But you said—"

"I know what I said."

"You mean you're going to keep me on in this job?"

"It might surprise you, but I do believe in second chances. Especially when there are extenuating circumstances for you."

Haley should have been upset that he'd acted out of pity again, but she was too busy being grateful that he'd changed his mind. "Thank you. You won't be sorry. I promise." Words rushed from her mouth as she hurried to reassure him before he changed his mind. "I'll keep my end of the bargain. You just write down Elizabeth's schedule, and I'll follow it."

"I'm sure you will."

Haley pressed on as if he still needed convincing. "And I'll follow your house rules, no matter how strict."

Matthew cocked his head to the side, drawing his eyebrows together. "You make me sound like a dictator instead of a father."

"Oh, no, no, no. I just mean I want you to know that you can trust me."

He looked over his shoulder at the child who had slept through the disagreement and its resolution before turning back to her. "I know I can."

She studied him to see if he was serious, and there was no humor in his eyes. Though she was thrilled that he'd decided to give her another chance, she didn't understand it. What had changed?

He answered her unasked question with a simple statement: "I love her, too."

It all made sense now. Because he knew she loved Elizabeth, he hoped she would do what was best for her. And he was right: she would.

The matter settled, Matthew opened his car door and stepped outside. Opening the rear door, he reached in and started unbuckling his daughter's car seat.

The child's lids opened, and she rubbed her eyes with her fists. "I want Miss Haley…" Her groggy voice slipped away as she drifted into her dreams again.

Haley climbed out, already starting toward his side of the car. "Do you need any help?"

"No. I've got it under control." He lifted Elizabeth carefully in his arms. "Thanks, though. I'll see you in the morning."

With a wave, Haley headed over to her car and unlocked the door. She felt as if she'd been given a gift rather than a brief reprieve from another round of unemployment. Not only had Matthew allowed her the opportunity to spend more time with his wonderful daughter, he'd taken a chance on Haley.

As she drove away, she wondered if he regretted his decision already or would by the time she arrived in the morning. She couldn't do anything about that, but there was one thing she could do. He'd given her another chance, and she would do whatever she could to deserve it.

Chapter Seven

~~

The next morning as Matthew knotted his tie in front of the mirror and smoothed the corners of his collar, he could hear Haley pulling her car into the drive. He still had a few minutes before he needed to be at the office, so he shrugged into his suit jacket, settled his briefcase in the hall and then went to meet her at the front door.

As he opened the door, he inhaled a deep breath of the crisp morning air. This would be a different day in his working relationship with Haley. A better day. It felt great to be in control, even if it was over only one small part of his life.

Haley smiled at him. "Good morning?"

Because she'd posed it as a question, he smiled back to reassure her. "Yes, it is." He pushed the door fully open and stepped back to allow her to enter.

Slipping off her tennis shoes, Haley padded to the closet with little white socks peeking out from beneath her jeans. She stowed her heavy-looking shoulder bag in the bottom of the closet and hung her coat on the rod, even facing it the same way as all of his coats and jackets.

As she turned back to him, he noticed that she'd topped off her outfit with a sweatshirt from Ball State University, one of the colleges from her varied journey of higher education. She looked young in that outfit, more like a playmate for Elizabeth than a caregiver, but as long as Haley followed their agreement from last night, it didn't matter what she looked like.

Haley scanned the living room and the portion of the kitchen visible from the entry. "Where is Elizabeth? Is she still sleeping?"

He glanced to the staircase and back down at Haley again. It was just as well that Elizabeth wasn't around for the start to this day. "I haven't even heard her move yet this morning. She was really tired."

Haley stared at the floor for a few seconds before straightening and planting her hands on her hips. "Okay, do you have any special instructions for me?"

Boy, did he ever. "Right in here."

He led her into the kitchen and, with a gesture of his hand, indicated two documents on the counter. One had the heading "Schedule" and the other bore the words "House Rules."

"Very detailed," she said as she started to lift the papers and found them secured to the counter. "Typed and taped, you've certainly been busy."

"I had a few free minutes."

Haley stood against the counter and read the second document aloud. "Number one, bed must be made before breakfast. Number two, teeth should be brushed immediately after breakfast. Number three, only healthy snacks between breakfast and lunch."

Until hearing his list read aloud, Matthew had been proud of both documents, products of his hard work at the computer. Now the words she read sounded silly. Even the schedule seemed over-the-top when last night he'd thought it was perfect.

Maybe he was the dictator that they'd joked about yesterday evening. "You know me. I can't do anything halfway."

"And you know me. I can't finish anything at all."

"That's not true," he said, more because he hoped it than that he believed the validity of it.

Haley turned her attention back to the lists on the counter. She read the rest of the rules silently and then perused the schedule, which blocked out time for everything from breakfast to mid-morning reading time. When she finished, she popped to attention and saluted him.

"Thank you, sir. I'll do my best, sir."

He'd never been the blushing type, but Matthew felt his face go warm. "All right. All right."

The project he'd been so proud of only embarrassed him now. Haley thought he was ridiculous. Was he raising a daughter or a military cadet? He was surprised Haley hadn't laughed out loud when she'd read his lists. She hadn't, and the more he thought about it, even the smile she'd given him when she saluted had rested only on her lips, never reaching her eyes.

Why hadn't he realized that his attempt to control every detail of her day with his daughter would hurt Haley's feelings? How could he tell her that he trusted her and then present her with an extensive list of rules that proved he didn't? Worse than that, he'd practically engraved them in the granite countertop like the stone tablets of the Ten Commandments.

Suddenly, he wanted to take it all back, to tell her that these were just guidelines instead of hard-and-fast rules. He wrestled with the words to say. He'd never been good at admitting he was wrong. A glance at his watch, though, told him he would have to backpedal later. Yes, later was good. That would give him time to come up with a good excuse for being a jerk because the concerned daddy defense only went so far.

Haley must have misunderstood his hesitation for worry because she put on what looked like a pasted smile. "Don't worry. I'll make you proud."

"I'm not worried. Really."

She raised a doubting brow that shamed him. "Well, good, then, because you have to get to work, don't you?"

Another glance at his watch proved her right. "You know, all this isn't really…" he began, but a pounding sound from upstairs stopped him from finishing.

"Somebody's finally coming to life this morning." Haley started down the hall to the stairs, speaking to him over her shoulder. "Now I'm sure you have clients to get to, so have a great day. Elizabeth and I have plenty to keep us busy. Our schedule's probably tighter than yours."

Because she continued toward the landing and started up the stairs, he couldn't see her face, but he figured she wasn't smiling. He couldn't blame her. He'd probably offended her on many levels.

Matthew crossed to the hall closet and grabbed his overcoat. He'd expected to feel invigorated and in control after this meeting, so he didn't know what to do with this empty feeling. The victory felt more like defeat.

As he collected his briefcase and exited through the garage, he could hear a squeal coming from upstairs. Elizabeth was obviously thrilled with the surprise of having Haley come to get her from her room instead of him. More squeals and giggles followed, so he could only guess that a tickle battle had ensued.

Didn't he want tickle battles for his daughter? And even messy, mural-making moments on rare, warm winter afternoons? Of course he did. Sure, he wanted stability and absolute security for his child, but he also wanted to entertain her imagination, to give her the opportunity to frolic and to offer her the chance to know joy.

So why had he just bound the hands of the person who, despite her flighty nature, seemed to live life more fully than anyone he'd ever known? Was it because joy wasn't something that he'd personally experienced in a long time and couldn't teach to his child? He didn't want to believe he felt threatened by Haley, but the facts didn't support his case.

The accusation of it chased him as he climbed in his car and backed out of the driveway. Before he pulled away, he cast one last glance at the blond brick colonial, his gaze drawn to the single, lighted window on the second floor. He wondered if Haley and Elizabeth were still wrestling on the bed or if Haley had already been forced to stop the fun to help Elizabeth begin her morning by making the bed. For his daughter's sake, he hoped the giggles would go on just a little longer.

* * *

Haley settled back into the pew with her mother and sisters on one side and Elizabeth and the majority of the Warren family on the other. She wasn't sure when Dylan and Logan had entered the sanctuary. Sometime between the opening prayer and the second verse of "The Garden," the two had suddenly filled the empty seats next to their mother.

"Miss Haley," Elizabeth said in a child's loud version of a whisper. "Uncle Dylan and Uncle Logan are here now. They're late."

She said the word "late" as if it contained two syllables. Haley leaned forward in her seat so she could give the two men a quick wave. Dylan waved back, keeping his hand low so not to be visible over the top of the pew. Logan grinned at her and winked.

Haley was smiling, too, until she looked to the front of the church again, and put on a straight face. Matthew was staring down at them from his music minister's bench; the tight flex of his jaw suggested he wasn't pleased. Unlike his brothers, who sported polo shirts and khaki slacks, Matthew wore a dark suit, crisp white shirt and crimson tie, his attire as serious as his expression.

Haley straightened in her seat and took hold of Elizabeth's hand again. She indicated with a tilt of her head that the child should pay attention to what was happening at the podium.

The last thing Haley wanted to do was cause the child to misbehave in church, especially after all of her hard work this week to establish a tentative peace with Matthew. Just thinking about how difficult it had been to fit Matthew's schedule around her own fun agenda made her feel exhausted again. Still, she was proud of the progress they'd made, and she didn't want to lose ground now.

As Reverend Boggs read the morning's announcements, Haley found herself sneaking glances at Matthew and his two brothers. She hadn't seen them in the same room together in years. It was no secret that the Warren brothers were as radically different in personality as she and her sisters, but these guys never had more than a basic family resemblance. Clearly, that hadn't changed.

Logan was still the family *pretty boy,* with bright green eyes instead of brown ones like his brothers' and dimples that some women probably fawned over. Matthew had neither the dimples nor Dylan's Greek-statue-type cheekbones, but his rounded baby face had always been appealing in its own way, perhaps in its surprising contrast to the hard lines of his demeanor.

At a touch on her left shoulder, Haley started, feeling guilty at being caught checking out guys in church, even if only for comparison's sake.

Jenna rested a comforting hand on Haley's shoulder, and Haley pressed her cheek against that hand. On the other side of Jenna, Caroline leaned forward and smiled.

Haley couldn't begin to measure how much she would miss her sisters when they left this afternoon, boarding flights back to their real lives. She would be left behind as the only one whose life had been forever changed by recent events.

Still, as much as she would miss "shopping therapy" with Jenna and board games with her mother and Caroline, Haley needed a break from all that togetherness. Their support came with the pressure of their expectations.

All week Jenna kept insisting that Haley should get back "out there" into the dating scene, though Jenna didn't seem to be all that "out there" herself lately. On the other hand, whenever Caroline wasn't dodging their mother's matchmaking efforts, she was sharing pearls of wisdom on why Haley shouldn't need a man in her life at all.

Matthew stepped to the lectern again, his commanding presence filling all the space around him. "Would you all please turn in your hymnals to page sixty-seven and join me in singing 'How Great Thou Art'?"

Releasing Elizabeth's hand, Haley reached for the book, the words of the hymn flowing through her thoughts before the pianist began the introduction. She appreciated how Matthew tended to favor more traditional hymns over the modern praise songs played in her church in Michigan. She enjoyed the new stuff, too, but there was just something about singing the old favorites and feeling that oneness with other Christians, who for hundreds of years had been using these same words to praise their God.

Haley could just imagine the blessings Matthew must enjoy from sharing these hymns with the congregation each week. She looked up from her hymnal expectantly after she'd sung the songwriter's opening lyrics about the awesome wonder he felt in God's presence.

Though Matthew's beautiful baritone voice flowed though the microphone, none of that awe showed on his face. Haley didn't know what to make of it. Didn't Matthew feel the anticipation when he sang of the writer's joy at the thought of Christ's return? Was Matthew so busy in his schedules and rules that he missed the messages contained in the songs he led?

Haley shook away the thoughts, admonishing herself that she was the one who should be listening to the messages. She didn't have the right to expect anyone else to react to hymns or even Scripture the same way she did. Only God could decide how He would speak to people's hearts.

Still, she couldn't help watching him and wondering about his church experience as she flipped to Reverend Boggs's Scripture text in Genesis 22. She hoped that all of Matthew's obligations as part-time music minister and member of the church finance and grounds committees didn't prevent him from finding time to have joy in simply praising God.

"In verse two," the minister began, "God tells Abraham 'Take your son, your only son Isaac, whom you love and go to the land of Moriah, and offer him there as a burnt offering….' Now you parents out there, try to imagine Abraham's quandary.

"Isaac was the son he and Sarah had dreamed about for decades. The child who was born when Abraham was one hundred years old and when Sarah was over ninety." Reverend Boggs shook his head for effect. "Can you imagine the agony Abraham must have felt when God asked him to sacrifice his precious son? And yet he didn't question. He followed God's instructions, preparing to take his son's life, until God told him to stop."

Haley skimmed the Old Testament words again, the Scripture story she'd heard so many times before sounding different today. No, she wasn't a parent. She could only imagine the love she would feel for her own child and the overwhelming pain she would feel to lose that child. Still, if the fiercely protective way she was beginning to feel about Elizabeth gave her a clue, that love would be all-encompassing and the loss, incomprehensible.

With her free hand, she slipped her arm around Elizabeth's tiny shoulders. As Haley settled her hand against her side, she couldn't resist peeking up at Matthew, who sat with a black leather Bible open across his lap. He was staring at the child next to her, stark emotions clear on his face. As if he sensed her watching, Matthew shifted his head slightly, and his gaze connected with Haley's.

At first Haley stiffened, and she wondered if she should sit away from Elizabeth, if Matthew thought she was distracting his daughter by holding her so close. But then a strange, warm look appeared on his face. Was it understanding that she read in his eyes? Did he realize that he wasn't the only one who cared deeply for his child?

"Yes, Abraham was willing to sacrifice what was most dear to him," Reverend Boggs continued. "Our Father usually asks far less of us, and yet for most of us, the sacrifice is still too great. What could you give up to do God's work? Your Sunday night TV dramas? Maybe the Wednesday night bowling league?"

Haley couldn't help smiling at the direction the minister's sermon was taking. By the time that the closing prayer was spoken, she'd already determined that if she gave up feeling sorry for herself, she would have plenty of time to do church work.

"Uncle Dylan. Uncle Logan." Elizabeth squeezed her way past her grandmother to reach the two men on the end of the pew once the service had concluded.

"Hey, munchkin," Logan said, swinging his niece up for a bear hug.

Dylan leaned in to kiss the child's cheek. "I've missed you too much."

After Logan lowered Elizabeth to her feet, he turned to hug his mother.

"What kept you two this morning?" Amy Warren said in a saccharine-sweet voice.

"Ask Logan," Dylan said drily. "Or better yet, don't."

Logan shrugged. "Why, Mom? Are you planning to sacrifice your children, just for being late to church?"

"Very funny," she said.

Trina, who had come around the other end of the pew, stepped up to her friend's sons. "She won't do that, but she probably knows why some animals eat their young."

Soon the Warren and Scott families—complete for the first time in a long time—were exchanging awkward hugs in the nearly empty sanctuary. Even Matthew had made his way back from the receiving line and was frowning at his brothers who'd been MIA all week.

The scene made Haley smile. It felt like a flashback to her childhood, to the time when she still believed that all stories had happy endings. Before any of them knew about divorces, deaths and failed engagements. It was so great having them all here together. Too bad this was only temporary as a couple of them had a flight to catch.

Chapter Eight

"I don't think it's going to work out."

Trina Scott had been stirring two sugar cubes into a cup of Earl Grey, but at her best friend's words, she set aside the cup from her favorite tea service.

"What are you talking about?"

Amy Warren rubbed one stocking-clad foot against the other and straightened the floral-print skirt she'd worn to church and then to the airport. Lifting her cup and saucer from the coffee table, she took a sip and lowered it again.

"You know what I mean," Amy said. "The plan."

Trina turned her head from side to side then grinned when she remembered they were alone. She didn't have to worry about anyone overhearing them. After she and Amy had returned with Haley from the airport, Haley had headed off on errands, giving the two friends a chance to chat.

Trina appreciated not having to be so careful with her words, at least for a while.

Earlier in the week, she and Amy had agreed to avoid continually mentioning their match-making plan in front of the others. A love match might be more likely to sneak up on their children if they weren't being so up front about their roles as catalysts for the intended happy developments.

She waved away Amy's worries with a brush of her hand. "When did you become such a naysayer?"

"I'm not a naysayer. It's just—"

"Just that you're being a Gloomy Gail. 'Oh ye of little faith.' Come on. We just haven't given our plan enough time to play out yet. These things take time. Caroline and Matthew are just getting to know each other."

Amy raised a brow but sipped from her cup again rather than making a cynical comment.

"You know what I mean," Trina said with a frown. "Sure, they *know* each other, but they're hardly acquainted at all as adults. They haven't had time to see the incredible people they've become."

Amy drew her eyebrows together. "I don't know."

"It might have been easier if Matthew weren't the only guy around all week. What really happened to Dylan and Logan, anyway?"

"I just can't figure those two out." With a huff, Amy folded her arms across her. "As you can tell, they've come out of hiding now that they know all the big family gatherings are over."

Trina nodded, sharing her friend's disappointment. "Even without their absence, this week wasn't exactly the perfect matchmaking moment. Especially with all that fuss to deal with over the wedding that never was."

"And never should have been," they said in chorus and laughed.

Trina turned to stare out the window, where the sky stretched in miles of gray. "Haley doesn't realize yet what a blessing she's been given. One of these days, though, she'll figure it out."

"She always does eventually."

Trina nodded. Her friend was right as she'd been about so many things over the years. Haley would find her way just as her sisters had. Only it would take her a little longer than the others. "At least Matthew and Haley worked out whatever differences they were having about Elizabeth's care."

"Did Haley tell you anything?"

"Not a word."

"These ungrateful children," Amy said. "Can't even give their long-suffering mothers a morsel of information when the story looked so interesting."

Trina's hand shook as she chuckled, causing the tea to slosh in her cup. She set it aside before she made a mess.

"That Matthew would be tight-lipped about

something shouldn't surprise either of us," Amy continued. "Stacey had been gone three weeks before I found out about it, and we lived across town."

"But Haley's been silent, too." Trina shook her head. "She hasn't kept a secret from me in her whole life. I even patted her on the shoulder a few times the other night, and I got nowhere."

"Boy, you *were* trying." A knowing smile played on Amy's lips.

Trina smiled back. Of course, her best friend knew how hard it was for her to be the soft, comforting mother. It just wasn't in her nature. How blessed she'd been to have a friend who knew her failings and loved her anyway.

"Elizabeth sure made her presence known at The Pie the other night." Amy grinned as she settled back in her chair. "The way Matthew looked at Haley, I thought he was going to fire her on the spot."

"Well, at least they worked it out. Haley needs something she can count on right now, and Matthew can stop worrying about child care long enough to look at his other personal options."

"Like your Caroline?"

"I like the way you think, sister."

Still, Amy took on a pensive look then. "Have you ever considered that they might not be right for each other?"

"Are you kidding? Have you ever *met* our two oldest children?" She tilted her head to the side, giving Amy her best look of incredulity. "God couldn't have made a pair with more in common than those two."

"You're right. But neither of them seemed that enthused with our hints."

"When have our children ever accepted our advice? At least the first time we gave it."

"Never."

"That's right," Trina said with a firm nod. "And I don't know about Matthew, but Caroline is stubborn enough to frustrate anyone. She's always had to do everything *her* way. I told her she would have made a lovely teacher or nurse, but, no. She just kept going on about her business plans and breaking glass ceilings."

"Jenna told me Caroline's on this kick about never marrying."

Trina rolled her eyes. "She thinks that's what she wants, but she'll change her mind when she finds the right man. And we both believe Matthew is the right man for her, don't we?"

"Of course we do. It's just that—I don't know. It seems like we might be pushing too hard."

"Or not hard enough. In biblical days, we would have made the deal before either of them was weaned."

"And I would own your cow now."

Trina shrugged. "You're right. Families with daughters didn't exactly make out during those times."

"Times have changed, too. Arranged marriages aren't in vogue anymore."

"Well, they should be," Trina said with a firm nod. "The divorce rate sure would be lower."

Leaning her elbow on the arm of the chair, Amy stared off into space before turning back to her friend. "When do you think *the plan* went from being just a joke to something we might be tempted to call serious?"

"When Matthew did such a poor job of choosing for himself and ended up miserable." Trina didn't even have to mention the fiasco of a marriage and divorce that poor Amy had suffered through, as well. Neither of them would ever wish that kind of pain on any of their children, and Amy's son had already experienced it.

"And *the plan* changed when Caroline refused to choose at all." Trina crossed her arms, settling back into the chair. "I don't even know what to say about the others. Just look at the king-size mistake Haley almost made, and the others don't seem any closer to making good decisions, either."

"We have to do something."

Amy hadn't been on board with their discussion, so Trina was pleased by her friend's change of heart. Infused with new energy, Amy scooted to the edge of her chair.

"Our kids need our help, but what we've tried so far hasn't worked," Amy said.

"Okay, so what will?"

"Up until now, most of our plans have been more like subterfuge."

"We have been pretty sly, haven't we?"

Amy nodded, on a roll now. "We need to step up our game. I'm going to tell Matthew he needs to ask Caroline on a date, and I'm going to tell him why."

Now it was Trina's turn for misgivings. "Are you sure that won't just put him off?"

"I've been honest and up front with him about everything else, haven't I?"

"Except in giving him child-rearing advice."

"Okay, except that. And he appreciates my restraint on that." Amy paused as if reclaiming her momentum. "Anyway, I'm going to suggest that he ask Caroline to dinner the next time she visits Markston."

"Have I mentioned how hard it is to get my firstborn to take any time off from work?"

"Well, you'll just have to insist that she visit her dear widowed mother more often. Tell her that she has a jilted younger sister who needs her company, too. That should soften her up some."

"Remind me never to get on your bad side, dear pal. You're good at getting your own way."

"God does give us special gifts, doesn't He?" Amy grinned.

"So what do we do if Matthew is too shy or…er…reluctant to ask Caroline out himself?"

"Oh, I wouldn't worry about that."

"Why is that? Not twenty minutes ago you weren't even certain we were doing the right thing or that things between those two would ever work out." Trina planted hands on the sides of her skirt and tilted her head.

"Well, twenty minutes ago I didn't have a plan." She held her hands wide. "Now I do."

From the sparkle in Amy's eyes, Trina could only guess that her friend had other ideas brewing, as well. This new enthusiasm was contagious, and anticipation ran through her veins. She was certain they'd be having a family wedding to celebrate before they knew it.

A squeal of glee caught Haley's attention as she rinsed the last of the lunch dishes, so she shut off the water. She and Elizabeth had some creating to do. The dishes could wait.

She approached the table where Elizabeth was building a fluffy white creation with a huge pile of shaving cream. Each day since her sisters had left, Haley had been coming up with creative activities to do with Elizabeth. She was especially proud of her plan this time as she'd packed a roll of wax paper and the can of shaving cream in the satchel of surprises she brought each morning.

Not only would shaving cream creations be fun, but, because she and Elizabeth had taped the wax paper to the table, the cleanup would be easy. The lime scent of the shaving cream would probably be harder to get rid of, but she'd cross that bridge when she reached it.

Elizabeth squealed again, and Haley smiled.

"What's that all about?" She glanced across the table where the child had squished the mound of creamy white into big globs and smeared imaginary roads all over the table.

"Look, Miss Haley. It's an igloo."

She bent so that her head was about level with the tabletop. Sure enough, there was a rounded mound of shaving cream with some sort of dent in the side. A door maybe?

"You're right. It's a wonderful igloo. Your fingers are probably freezing just building it."

"Ooh, it's cold." Elizabeth shivered and then giggled. She was wearing a sweater because her father liked to keep the heat low in the house, but she was unlikely to need a parka anytime soon.

"Can you see the Eskimos?" Elizabeth asked her.

Haley studied the creation for a few seconds longer. Unless those smaller lumps around the bigger lump were the dwelling's inhabitants, she didn't see them.

"I know *you* do," she said finally and was pleased to find that her young charge accepted that answer.

"You can't see all of the Eskimos," Elizabeth said importantly, "because they're inside having tea."

"With crumpets, I hope."

The child nodded. Her smile made all the effort to create little projects like this one worthwhile. Haley loved that Elizabeth still had a child's imagination, where clouds could be mountain ranges and where a tent made of old quilts could be a spaceship to Mars. She had many years ahead to learn life's realities, so Haley wanted to encourage her to enjoy the innocent optimism of childhood for as long as she could.

"What else do you think I can make? What about the *Adominable* Snowman?"

Haley laughed. "Do you mean the *Abominable* Snowman?"

Elizabeth cocked her hip and planted a sticky hand on side of her jeans. "You know, the one with Rudolph?"

She glanced at the clock that had not been her friend lately. "You might have to wait until next time because you have to cleanup now for your rest time."

"Oh, can't we play a little longer?"

"Sorry. It's important that you get a little rest, so you'll be all ready to have fun when your daddy gets home."

"But I'm not tired."

"Well, that's wonderful because you'll have more time to read books in your bed." Already, Haley had learned that the more positive a spin she put on the afternoon schedule, the easier it was to accomplish.

"Just a few more minutes."

"Okay. Five." Haley smiled to herself. At least she'd remembered this time to build a little extra time into this process so she could "give in" for a few minutes and keep with the schedule.

"Yippee!"

Elizabeth picked this moment to slap both hands on the table, wreaking creamy white havoc on her igloo and all of its inhabitants. Unfortunately, the shaving cream also landed with multiple splats on the wall, the other dining chairs, the hardwood floor, even the oval-shaped rug beneath the table.

"Uh-oh."

"Yeah. Uh-oh, Lizzie. I mean Elizabeth." Haley pulled a glob of shaving cream from her own hair, while glancing at the spattering of white dotting the child's braids. So much for her amazing idea for fun with an easy cleanup.

"Daddy's going to be mad."

"Of course he won't. We'll just get it all cleaned up before he gets home." She didn't even delude herself with the hope that Matthew wouldn't learn the whole story later. He did live with a four-year-old reporter after all. "Here, let me wet some washcloths."

She hurried over to the sink and put a few cloths under the faucet. A noise from behind her caught her attention, so she glanced back over her shoulder to find that they weren't alone. Matthew stood just inside the door with his arms crossed.

Swallowing hard, Haley shut off the faucet, wrung out the cloths and turned to face him. "Hi, Matthew."

"Daddy!" Then, as if she'd just remembered the mess that surrounded her, Elizabeth added, "Oh."

"Right. Oh," he repeated.

Haley grabbed the rags and headed back to the table. "Look, we just had a bit of an accident here, and we're hurrying to clean it up so Elizabeth will be on time for her—"

"Here. Let me help."

Haley opened her mouth and then closed it. She didn't know what she'd expected him to say, but it wasn't that. Probably something about messes and lack of responsibility. Definitely not this. She stared at his outstretched hand before finally thinking to pass him a cloth. She put another cloth in Elizabeth's hands.

"Hey, sorry about this. It's only shaving cream. We'll get it cleaned up. Really."

But Matthew didn't seem to be listening. He

was bending instead, his suit jacket draping forward, as he wiped white globs from the bright yellow kitchen wall. Across the room, his daughter was smearing circles of shaving cream on the formerly shiny hardwood.

Haley settled on her hands and knees and started scrubbing the rug. With each swipe, the mess foamed more, and another whiff of lime filled her nostrils. Would this stuff ever come out?

Finally, Matthew stood up again. He stepped over to the table and leaned closer, studying the mess that remained on the wax paper.

Elizabeth scrambled to her feet, her cloth dangling from her fingers. "I'm sorry, Daddy. We were just having fun and..." She chewed her lip and stared at the floor.

"Hey, why the sad face?"

Matthew reached her in two long strides and awkwardly messed with her bangs. The tenderness of the moment squeezed Haley's heart.

"I was just admiring some of your artwork." He waited until she looked up at him before continuing. "What were you building here before the...er...explosion?"

"Igloo," Elizabeth mumbled.

"I'm sure it was a great...uh...igloo."

"It sure was," Haley agreed.

Haley was tempted to say more, to rave about Elizabeth's creations, but she kept quiet instead and continued to scrub the rug. This was Matthew's time with his child, not hers, and even if he felt uncomfortable with imaginative play, he was trying.

She continued to watch as Matthew followed Elizabeth around the table and patiently listened while she described her artistic vision. It couldn't have been more endearing. Haley had always thought Matthew was handsome, but to her, he'd never been more attractive than he was right now, simply being daddy to his little girl.

"I messed up my igloo." Elizabeth pointed to the spot where her structure had once stood. "I made a mess, too. It was supposed to be clean."

"Messes are okay sometimes, especially when you're having fun," Matthew told her. "Were you having fun?"

She nodded. "Miss Haley said I needed to stop because it was time to rest. I didn't want to stop."

"I know. Maybe next time you can play longer with the shaving cream. Why don't you head upstairs and read while Miss Haley and I finish cleaning this up?"

"Okay, Daddy." With a hug and a kiss for him and for Haley, she headed toward the stairs.

That left Haley alone in the kitchen with Matthew. The last time they'd been alone in there, just over a week before, he'd shown her his list of mandates taped to the counter. Although he'd moved those documents—they could be found hanging from the side of the refrigerator with a magnet—that didn't mean the rules had changed. Haley braced herself for the worst, which was what it would be if he decided she couldn't be with Elizabeth anymore.

Chapter Nine

Matthew watched as Haley sat crisscross on the floor and continued to work on the mess. Having already wiped the remaining spots from the wall, he walked to the sink to rinse his washcloth. She was still scrubbing when he stepped back over to her. Was she that worried about what he planned to say?

"This place is going to smell like lime air freshener for a long time, don't you think?"

At his words, Haley's hand stilled. "Really, Matthew, I'm sorry."

"Lime's not a bad smell." He waited for her to look up at him before he continued. "Definitely better than that menthol stuff."

"That's what I thought."

He moved over to the table and started to lift the wax paper only to find it secured with tape. Just like his list of rules had been. "So, what was the plan here?"

Haley twisted out of her seated position and stood, resting her hand on the table's edge. "Supposedly to keep the table clean and be an easy cleanup." Her smile held as much irony as her words.

"Well, you know what? That table still looks clean."

Her smile made him wish he'd said something funny a whole lot earlier.

"Unfortunately, the table's the only clean thing."

"Nothin' a few hands and some elbow grease can't fix."

Haley stared at him, appearing surprised by his uncharacteristic use of slang. "Wait. Was that Matthew? If I didn't know better, I'd say that was your mother talking. Or mine."

"Our two mothers are pretty wise women overall."

She crouched down again, going after a blob next to the table leg. "You mean about *the plan?*"

"Except for that."

"You've got to give them credit for trying."

"I guess."

"At least they have your best interests at heart." She carried her washcloth over to the sink and rinsed it.

"Now don't you start."

"Don't worry. This is a matchmaking-free zone."

"Whew." He gave his brow an exaggerated swipe. "I was ready to run for my car."

"They are right though. Caroline is a great person."

Matthew glanced at her, but when he didn't find the mischief in her eyes that he'd expected, he nodded. What she said about her sister was true. He couldn't think of a clever way to respond to that, either, so he reached under the table and began unfastening the tape. Haley did the same thing on the other end. Soon they were rolling the two ends of the paper together, easily keeping that part of the mess inside.

When Matthew had all the paper in a ball, Haley grabbed the trash can from beneath the sink, and he stuffed the ball inside it.

"See." Matthew indicated the table with a nod. "A perfectly clean table."

"Great," she said without enthusiasm.

Haley plopped down on the floor and started on a new section of the rug. Matthew hung his suit jacket on one of the dining chairs, grabbed his cloth again and worked on the spots that dotted the sideboard. For a few minutes, they worked companionably to restore the kitchen.

Finally, Haley's head popped up. "Hey, you never said why you're home in the middle of the day."

"I had this sudden need for a good shave."

"It's definitely important to be clean-shaven in court," Haley agreed but then tilted her head, studying him. "So you're sure you weren't just checking up on us? Maybe seeing if we were jumping off the roof to test the law of gravity?"

Matthew shook his head. "Have I dropped in to check up any other day?" Though he emphasized his point, his smile was probably too wide for her not to notice. Checking up on them wasn't his motivation for coming today, and he'd prefer that she not know about those times last week when he'd been tempted to do just that.

She moved her head from side to side as if considering his question. "No. I guess not. But maybe you just couldn't get away, and you would have checked up on us before."

If it were possible for his smile to widen, Matthew was sure it would have. Haley Scott was a clever woman. He must learn not to underestimate her.

"Okay, you're at least partially right. This is the first time I could get away, but I didn't come to check up on you two." Glancing around to ensure that they'd cleaned the last of the mess, he reached for the cloth in her hand and carried his and hers into the laundry room just off the kitchen.

When he returned, he added, "I came to see what you two were doing."

"Can you explain to me how those two things are different?"

"I just wanted to see what fun activities you'd planned for today." He opened the refrigerator door and collected the makings of a turkey and provolone sandwich before leaning out again. "You always have some kind of exciting event planned."

"How did you—"

"You didn't expect a four-year-old to be able to keep a secret, did you? I've been getting the play-by-play every night. The A-B-C clay monsters, Princess and one hundred peas, those amazing pairs on Noah's ark. She's told me about all of them."

At first, he'd been a little jealous of both Haley's creativity and the fact that Elizabeth was so enamored with her, but now he just appreciated that someone was making such an effort to make learning fun for his daughter.

Haley's cheeks reddened, but she didn't look away from him. "I guess I don't have any secrets, then."

"You're like Mary Poppins with that satchel of yours. It has as many surprises as her carpetbag. I'm beginning to expect you to pull a floor lamp out of it soon."

"I doubt I can do that."

"But you've done something even more important with your fun approach to learning. You've convinced Elizabeth that she should try preschool in the fall. She wasn't ready earlier this year."

Her smile and her pretty blush made everything he'd said seem worthwhile. He was tempted to say more, just to keep her smiling that way, so he focused on making his sandwich. He offered her one, as well, but she'd already eaten with Elizabeth, precisely at noon, as the schedule required. Trying not to feel guilty over that, he asked her to join him while he ate, and she took a seat opposite him at the dinette.

When he looked up from saying grace, Haley was watching him.

"Maybe I am a little like Mary Poppins. 'Practically perfect in every way.'" She chuckled over her own joke.

"Elizabeth sure thinks so."

He understood that Haley had been kidding, and he'd just been playing along, but Matthew was surprised by how tempted he was to agree with his daughter. In a lot of ways, particularly those that involved Elizabeth, Haley was "practically perfect."

The fact that he was beginning to think so worried him, so he pushed away the errant thought. He needed to remind himself that this particular Mary Poppins was also known for her

Peter Pan complex. She considered growing up something other people did, and while the rest of the world had to work in jobs even when they hated them, Haley never stuck to any long enough to have business cards made.

Sure, she might have put more effort into her activities than any of Elizabeth's other child-care providers, but Haley would never be around long enough to see the success of her efforts.

"I'm sorry I made Elizabeth late for her nap again," she said, clearly misunderstanding the meaning of his pause.

"There's no reason to apologize. I'm the one who should apologize for being so rigid about the schedule and the rules. I get caught up in the details sometimes."

"Ya think?" She stopped, looking wide-eyed. "I mean, you think so?"

"Okay, that's fair."

"No." Haley closed her eyes, shaking her head. "That's not what I meant."

"So, what did you mean? That my schedule and list of rules were over-the-top? That a few house rules and general schedule guidelines would have been plenty?"

"You said those things, not me."

She looked as if she was trying to keep a straight face, but the ends of the straight line of her lips slipped upward, and then she started giggling. Not a laugh like he would have expected from an adult woman but a youthful giggle. A strangely contagious one, too.

Soon Matthew found himself laughing right along with her. At himself, no less. He was surprised by how good it felt. Most of the time, he didn't have the luxury of taking himself less seriously. Too many people, too many things, were relying on him. He couldn't afford to fail.

When she finally stopped laughing, Haley rested her hands on the table and gave him a steady look. "Okay, maybe the lists were a bit…er…painstaking, but you had every right to make them. It's your house. Your child. You were just doing what you felt you had to—"

"To be the one in control," he finished for her.

She started shaking her head, but he continued, anyway. "You might not know this about me, but I'm a control freak."

One side of Haley's mouth lifted, but she didn't say anything clever. If they were discussing her negative personality traits, he doubted he would have shown the same restraint. He certainly hadn't before.

Pushing back from the table, he crossed to the refrigerator where the rules and the schedule were hanging from separate magnets. He pulled them both lose and ripped them in half. When he looked back to the table, Haley was watching him.

"I'm not suggesting that there should be no rules in this house," he explained, "but it wasn't necessary to post them like edicts. You know my general expectations. Beyond that, I'd just like you to use your judgment."

"Why the change of heart?"

"I overreacted." He returned to the table, carrying the torn papers with him. "We both know that. Yet, you followed all the rules and deadlines without complaining and still managed to squeeze in time for fun. I realized I don't need any lists to know you have my daughter's best interests at heart."

Haley lifted the remnants of the two torn documents. "So just how hard was it for you to get rid of these?"

He waved away her question. "Not hard." Then he stopped. "Okay, a little hard. I like to have all my ducks in a row, and I want all the mallards separated from the domestic varieties, too. I like plans, deadlines and boundaries. Could there ever be a person better suited to practice law?"

"There's nothing wrong with wanting to be in control of your life, Matthew."

He shrugged. "I guess as long as you realize that you're not ever really in control."

"There's an old saying that if you really want to make God laugh, tell Him your plans," she said.

Finishing the last bite of his sandwich, Matthew

pushed his plate aside. "I didn't get that. I figured as long as I did the right things, jumped through the right hoops, then my life would turn out differently than—"

Matthew stopped himself. What was he doing? It wasn't like him to spill his guts to anyone about Stacey or his father, so why was he tempted to make Haley the first? Sure, she could relate to the experience of rejection, but she couldn't understand what it felt like for a father to fail his child, how emasculating it felt to not be able to protect Elizabeth from people who would hurt her.

He stared at her and waited. If she were anything like either of their mothers, she would be pressing him for details before he had time to exhale.

Finally, he couldn't resist his curiosity. He looked up to find her studying him. Her eyes were so warm. So wise. She didn't ask him to say more, but she seemed to understand him almost too well, more than her own experiences should have taught her.

"You know," she said, taking an exaggerated pause, "one good thing about never having any plans for your life is that you always get to be surprised."

"I've never thought of it that way." Matthew smiled. She'd let him off the hook, and he was grateful. Maybe it had been wrong of him to always think of Haley as not quite a grown-up. She had grown into a kind, perceptive woman.

"Planning for a whole new life outlook?"

"You know me. You can't teach an old dog new tricks."

"You're not an old dog. Only twenty-eight in human years though I'm afraid it's far older in dog years."

"That's one hundred ninety-six."

"Okay, I take it back. You are an old dog."

"Thanks."

"You're welcome." Haley grinned but then her expression became serious. "I sure hope old dogs can change when they really need to. I know I'm trying."

Matthew glanced at her, but she was studying her hands. He wasn't sure what she was trying to tell him. It could have been anything from a decision to choose a more reliable fiancé to finally picking a career she liked enough to stick with it.

"Your mom told me that you're thinking of going back to school again," he said, hoping she would clue him in.

"I put aside my plans to earn my MFA—that's a master's in fine arts—when I became engaged. I'd always had this silly dream of being a writer." She shrugged, staring at the table. "Anyway, I've been accepted to the program at Indiana University, but now I'm not sure I still want it."

"Why not?"

Looking up at him, she smiled. "I'm feeling differently about it now that I've found work that I really enjoy. Elizabeth's just amazing."

Matthew didn't know if she was trying to reassure him or warn him with her words. Hadn't she once had a dream of being an accountant or something, followed by a list of other dreams?

Maybe she was having fun playing dollhouse with his daughter right now, but in another week she would probably start waffling again and realize she needed a new adventure. He couldn't sit back and wait for that day. He hadn't seriously been looking for a permanent replacement lately, but he needed to step up the search as soon as he had a free minute. Whenever that would be.

He looked at the clock, tightening his jaw with the realization that, as usual, his life was controlled by it instead of the other way around. "I need to get back to work. I have to be in court at three, and it's probably going to be a long one."

Haley stood, as well, taking his plate from him and carrying it to the dishwasher. She turned back just as he shrugged into his suit jacket.

"You never answered my earlier question. Not really. If you weren't checking up on us, then why are you home in the middle of the day?"

"I just had a little free time, and I—"

She shook her head, not buying it. "You pack a

lunch every day, and you happened not to pack one today on the off chance you'd have some free time?"

He held up both hands, caught. "All right. Guilty."

"Then why?"

"I didn't want to miss out on the fun."

In the preschool class that next Sunday morning, children were waving palm branches much the way Matthew imagined the people of Jerusalem might have as Jesus made his triumphant entrance into the city. Okay, he doubted the multitudes mentioned in the Gospels were using the branches as samurai swords the way these kids were. Just another Palm Sunday tradition.

"Okay now. Let's put down the palms."

As he stood in the classroom's open doorway, Matthew turned at the sound of a surprising but familiar voice. At the front of the class, Haley motioned to stop the frenzy around her. Matthew was shocked to see her there. She'd only been in Markston a few weeks and wouldn't be around long, and yet here she was volunteering to teach Sunday school.

When she caught sight of Matthew, she gave him a quick wave before turning back to the children.

"Does anybody remember what we were supposed to do with the palms?"

"Lay them down for the donkey and the baby donkey to walk on," Elizabeth called out.

"That's right," Haley said, nodding enthusiastically. "The people of Jerusalem laid clothes on the road and then cut branches and spread them on the ground for Jesus to come into the city."

As the samurai swords came up for battle again, she drew attention to the front of the room. "Who remembers what the people said to Jesus when he came into the city?"

"Hosanna!" several children called out at once.

Haley pointed to the white board behind her where she reviewed the words of Matthew 21:9b: "Hosanna to the Son of David! Blessed is he who comes in the name of the Lord! Hosanna in the Highest!"

Asking her students to lay their palm branches on the floor, Haley led a quick prayer and dismissed the children. She and the other teacher, who had been cleaning up spilled juice while Haley finished teaching, asked the children to line up by the classroom entrance and handed them off to their parents one by one. Each child gave her a big hug before heading out the door.

Elizabeth was last in line. "Hi, Daddy. Look at the picture I made." She shoved a large piece of tracing paper into his hands. The shape on it was obviously a palm that she'd placed under her paper, but she'd created her version by coloring over that texture with orange and purple crayons.

"That's nice." He turned to Haley, who handed Elizabeth's coat to him. "I didn't expect to see you here."

"It's something new," she said unnecessarily.

"You do know they can't read, right?" He indicated the Scripture she'd written on the white board.

"I know, but they like to pretend they can." She glanced back at the words she'd written in block letters. "They really liked the word *hosanna*."

He nodded. His curiosity piqued, he couldn't help asking, "How did you end up teaching in here?"

"I've been looking for a way to do my part in the church. I thought it would be fun to teach the little ones, so I volunteered to substitute." She shrugged. "I guess they needed me right away."

"So it's temporary, then." That made sense to him. Just another short-term project in a life that had been filled with them.

Out of the corner of his eye, he noticed Elizabeth putting down her drawing and moving over to the white board. A marker had been left out, so she grabbed it and started drawing on the board.

"It's not necessarily only temporary." Haley's gaze followed his daughter, as well, but then she looked back to Matthew. "One of the teachers is pregnant with her first child, and she would like to take some time off, so they've been looking for a replacement."

"Oh." He noticed she hadn't said "permanent," but then *permanent* probably didn't mean the same to Haley that it did to others.

"This was the perfect time to start though."

"Why do you say that?"

"Are you kidding?" She looked at him as if he'd just grown a third ear or something. "It's the Easter season. What a wonderful time of year for Christians."

He had to chuckle at her enthusiasm. "For those of us in the church business, Easter is another working weekend. We work overtime. Somebody has to put together all those wonderful services that everyone loves to attend. Good Friday, the Easter sunrise service, the main Easter service. Somebody has to plan all the vocal and instrumental selections."

As he was speaking, Haley had lifted her hand to her chin, and now she was holding it between her thumb and forefinger. Her gaze flicked to his daughter and back to him. "Are you always this cynical?"

"I'm not," he began, but he stopped himself because there was no way to answer that. He was, in fact, always this cynical. He'd just never had anyone call him on the fact before.

He'd also never seen Haley angry before. Hurt, yes, but never angry. Still, he could tell by the flex of her jaw that she was. "I'm sorry. I didn't mean that."

She just stared at him, not believing him. Her disbelief made him question himself. Was he really so jaded that he'd lost the true meaning in Christ's death and resurrection? No, that couldn't be true.

Haley glanced over at Elizabeth again, perhaps to make sure she wasn't listening.

"I know you probably didn't mean that the way you said it," she said. "I just hope you find time in all your 'overtime' to remember to thank God that the tomb was empty."

Chapter Ten

Haley bustled around the living room in Matthew's house nearly a week later, making sure everything was perfect. All the other rooms had been tidied, the table had been set and dinner such as it was, would be going in the water once it boiled.

A smile settled on her lips as she pictured herself wearing high heels and a frilly apron over her dress as she handed Matthew his slippers and newspaper when he came though the door. She could do the June Cleaver thing, right? But the fantasy crumbled as soon as Haley touched the rocker/recliner that moved to reveal a bunch of rubbery legs from dolls peeking out from under it.

She crouched and started pulling dolls, clothed in party dresses, from beneath the recliner-turned-dollhouse.

"Elizabeth," she called out to the child she'd

just heard on the stairs. "Someone forgot her dolls in here. Do you know who that someone might be?"

"Me."

Haley was reaching to see if there were any stragglers still beneath the chair when the splashing sound of water boiling over filtered in from the kitchen. Standing, Haley brushed her hands off on her un-June Cleaver-esque jeans. She jogged into the kitchen. She pulled the pan off the stove just as Elizabeth sprinted into the room.

"Miss Haley, the water's boiling over."

"I can see that."

The water would need to be cleaned up from the range's drip pan later but for now she still needed to cook dinner, so she placed the saucepan under the faucet to refill it.

Haley sighed as she returned to the living room. She wasn't anywhere near the 1950s TV character that had set an unattainable image for housewives. Haley's hair wasn't properly coiffed, her fuzzy slippers didn't give even an extra quarter-inch of height and her cooking wasn't close to gourmet. She did, however, have something in common with Barbara Billingsley, the actress who portrayed old June: they were both playacting.

Haley shook her head. No one actually still wanted a life like that, anyway, did they? "When did I become so un-PC?"

"What's PC?" Elizabeth asked from the other room.

"It stands for 'politically correct,'" she answered.

"Oh." Elizabeth didn't sound all that interested in the subject.

Haley hoped the child wouldn't press for a more detailed explanation, not when Haley was so busy getting her head on straight over other matters. She had no business daydreaming about Matthew Warren and his daughter as if they could become some quaint little family or something. Her relationship with Matthew was employee to employer. If she was blessed to become Matthew's friend, as well, that would be great, but it wasn't the most important thing. Caring for Elizabeth was.

Even that was only temporary.

Haley's heart squeezed over the thought as she glanced at the child sitting on the floor. Elizabeth was already playing again with the dolls she was supposed to be putting away. How could Haley bear to ever leave that sweet little girl or the child's father, who needed Haley more than he realized?

Matthew had asked her to commit for only thirty days, and they were already into the third week of their agreement. Time was ticking away too quickly. He'd already told her he would be seeking a permanent replacement. She should be looking for another job for that eventuality, but she couldn't bring herself to search the want ads. She wanted *this* job, wanted to work with *this* child, and she wanted to do it for as many years as they needed her.

For the first time in her life, she was doing something important. It didn't even matter that she was using little of the formal learning she'd gained in her long and varied higher-education process. She'd never felt more valuable in any of her other jobs, the ones that were supposed to offer growth potential. Elizabeth Warren had all kinds of *growth potential,* and Haley wanted to be there to share in all of it.

Maybe Matthew would even let her have that opportunity. He'd already said he trusted her to care for Elizabeth, and she suspected it was hard for him to trust anyone. She wanted to honor that trust by giving Elizabeth the best care she knew how.

Haley was invested in this family. Sometimes when she was playing with Elizabeth, she forgot, at least for a few seconds, why she'd returned to Markston and her homelessness and lack of employment that had forced her to stay. Now she *wanted* to stay.

If only she could convince Matthew to keep her on as Elizabeth's permanent caregiver, the situation would be great for all involved. Earlier today, she had an idea how to make her case: she would make herself indispensable to him by doing some household duties in addition to providing child care. When Matthew had called earlier to say he was stuck in court for the evening, she'd decided to put her plan into action.

Only now she was having second thoughts, particularly since her June Cleaver daydream had fallen flat. Just because she and Elizabeth had fallen into a natural relationship didn't mean she had the skills to be a domestic engineer.

The cooking was great in theory. Too bad she'd had so little practice at it. She regretted having always taken a restroom pass every time her mother tried to conduct a home-cooking class. Haley was a master of ordering takeout, but somehow she doubted that would impress Matthew.

No more time for second thoughts, she decided, as she heard Matthew's car in the drive. Even if keeping this job mattered more than she'd ever thought any job should, all she could do was present her case. The rest would be up to him.

Matthew scraped the remaining cheesy pasta noodles off the bottom of the saucepan where they'd burned to a nasty brown. Though he wondered if it was going to take a belt sander to clean the bottom of the pan, he was determined not to laugh. He'd managed to choke down two whole servings of her dinner of boxed macaroni combined with canned tuna and frozen peas, even though it tasted like a barbecue gone wrong.

All through dinner, he'd been praying that God would keep Elizabeth quiet so she wouldn't announce that dinner was terrible and refuse to eat it. The child had only said that it tasted funny and then had eaten all of her small serving, so Matthew considered it an answer to prayer.

Haley might not be the best cook in the world, but she'd earned an E for "effort" tonight. He appreciated that effort, too. For one day, he hadn't been responsible for everything. He'd been able to pull up a chair and dig into a meal he didn't have to cook. Okay, the food had been barely edible, but it was the thought that counted, and it counted for a lot.

"Daddy, I'm all clean," Elizabeth said as she rode into the room on Haley's back. The child was dressed warmly in her lavender footed pajamas, and her damp hair was combed back from her face.

It hardly surprised Matthew that the two of them charged into the room as a horse and jockey. This was the Haley he'd come to know over the past few weeks. If Haley and his daughter had *not* been playing a game of pretend when they returned from Elizabeth's bath, that would have surprised him more.

"I sank boats in the bathtub," his daughter announced as Haley lowered her to the ground.

"That sounds like fun." He couldn't help smiling as he watched them together, the horse and rider both caught in a fit of giggles.

Haley looked just the same as she did most days, wearing one of her many college sweatshirts—this time it read "Indiana State"—but somehow she seemed different to him tonight. Was she truly different, or had he changed in how he viewed her?

Strangely though, what he first had described as flightiness seemed more like spontaneity now, and the immaturity he'd pointed out before, he would now be tempted to call a fun-loving spirit. Had he softened? He wasn't sure, but he did realize he'd been too quick to judge her.

The thought that he might be attracted to Haley teased him, but he squashed it. Even if he was in the market for a relationship and even if their families weren't too close for him to risk the awkwardness of a potential breakup, he still wouldn't choose someone like Haley. Someone too similar to his ex-wife for him to ever trust her to stick around. Even if she didn't decide to go back to college as she was considering, she would find some other adventure to take her away from Markston.

If either of those things weren't enough to push his risky thoughts right out of his mind, then he had only to think of Elizabeth. Her needs had to come first. No matter what feelings he might be tempted to have for Haley, he couldn't risk allowing Elizabeth to be hurt when Haley left. And she would leave.

"Here, let me help you with that." Haley started pushing up her sleeves as she came behind him.

He had been scraping the pan into the garbage, but he shoved the can back below the sink and closed the cabinet door. Pouring some liquid soap into the pan, he filled it with suds.

"No, you cooked. Anyway, I'm about finished. This just needs to soak."

"Are we going to make Easter eggs tonight, Daddy?"

Elizabeth already had the refrigerator door open and was pulling out a carton of eggs.

"Hey, wait a minute," Matthew called out, but Haley beat him to his daughter, deftly removing the carton from the child's hands.

"Whoa. We want to be careful, or we'll drop those," she said.

"Sorry, sweetie." He shook his head, wiping his hands on a towel. "Not tonight. It's already too late, and you have to get to bed."

"But you promised," Elizabeth wailed.

Matthew steadied himself, determined to keep the upper hand in the situation. "Yes, I promised that we'll paint Easter eggs sometime before Easter Sunday. I didn't promise to do it tonight."

He waited for Haley to argue with him, to suggest that he give in to his daughter's demands, but she only put the eggs back in the refrigerator and closed the door.

"I guess you have some decisions to make in the next few days so you'll be ready to color eggs," Haley told her. "Like whether you want to have solid-colored eggs or striped eggs. And whether you'd like to draw designs on the eggs before you dye them. Maybe if you'll want to use stickers or stamps."

"Wow, I didn't realize there were so many choices," he said. No matter what thoughts he'd been having about Haley, he couldn't help being impressed by how easily she had distracted his daughter from her frustration by offering her limited choices. Some of the techniques for dealing with children that he'd learned by trial and error came so easily to Haley.

"I want stripes," Elizabeth said finally, her lip still quivering.

"You take your time," Matthew said, playing along with Haley. "But while you're thinking, you should also decide whether you want to color eggs here or at Grammy's."

Elizabeth didn't skip a beat. "Can Miss Haley color eggs with us?"

Matthew swallowed. No, this wasn't the way this conversation was supposed to go.

"Please, Daddy. It will be fun."

What was he supposed to say now? He was willing to risk the tantrum Elizabeth might throw if he shot down her idea, but if he did say no, it might suggest that he was uncomfortable being around Haley himself. He wasn't ready to admit that. He tried another tack instead.

"I'm sure she'll be too busy for that…with the wedding gifts she still needs to return and all." It didn't seem nice reminding Haley of her wedding, but a man had to do what a man had to do. "We can ask her though."

"Do you want to, Miss Haley?"

"I'd love to." Haley grinned at the child before turning to Matthew. "Oh, didn't I tell you that we finished shipping all the gifts by the time my sisters went home? Our mother didn't want to offend Miss Manners with any delay."

"Oh. Well, good, then." He wondered if Miss Manners would appreciate his invoking thoughts of Haley's broken engagement in order to avoid a social situation. He didn't feel all that great about it.

He reached down to brush Elizabeth's damp hair. "It's time for you to go to bed, little missy."

The whine he was conditioned to expect came right away, but Matthew scooped his daughter up and headed toward the stairs. Stopping as he crossed from the kitchen to the hall that led to the stairs, he turned back to Haley.

"Hey, if you want to wait a few minutes, we can have coffee or something."

At Haley's surprised expression, he added, "I just thought it would be nice to have some adult conversation."

She appeared skeptical, but she nodded anyway. Perhaps guilt was a part of his invitation, but he found he didn't regret it. Haley had been nice to make dinner for his family, and he wanted to make it up to her. Of course he couldn't allow himself to be attracted to her, but it was about time that he was more of a friend to her.

Chapter Eleven

Haley glanced up when Matthew returned to the kitchen, and she gripped her mug of coffee to warm her hands. "How did it go?"

"She was out like a light." He snapped his fingers. "Thanks for staying."

"I like adult conversation as much as the next gal," she said with a shrug.

He gestured toward the coffee machine. "I see you already made coffee."

"I figured I'd make myself useful. It's decaf. I don't know about you, but I don't want to be up all night. I have enough trouble sleeping lately."

His intense stare then made her feel uncomfortable. Just what had he seen when he'd looked so deeply?

With her fingertip, Haley traced the rose pattern on the side of her cup. "Nice dishes."

"Wedding gifts. When your spouse takes off

and leaves no forwarding address, you get to keep everything."

"Oh, bonus," she said without enthusiasm.

Finally, he took a sip of his coffee. "Hey, this is good. Really good."

"Surprised?" she couldn't help asking.

"No. It's just that it's decaf and…" He let his words end abruptly as she sat grinning at him.

"Don't worry about it. I know my coffee's better than my cooking."

"What are you talking about? The dinner you made was perfectly—"

"Lousy?"

"No, it was—"

"Terrible? Nauseating?"

Matthew frowned at her. "If you would stop interrupting me, I would have the chance to say that it was perfectly fine."

"If you've been held hostage for six months and haven't eaten anything but rice and water."

"I was thinking more of if you've had a crazy day at work, it was nice to come home to a cooked meal."

Haley opened her mouth, but she couldn't think of a way to answer that.

He threw his hands wide. "Okay, I admit it. Yours wasn't the best dinner I've ever eaten, but I do appreciate the effort. I also appreciate that the house looks great, too. Thanks for that."

"You noticed?"

"Of course I noticed. I'm a detail man. Well, I usually am."

She studied him for a few seconds, his comment seeming odd. "Why do you say that?"

"I've been too caught up in my own child-care drama and schedules to even think about what a tough time you've been going through lately."

"I'm okay."

"I just thought that you might be ready to talk about what happened to someone besides your mother and sisters."

Haley tilted her head to the side, his interest surprising her. "You mean to someone who isn't going to say I told you so?"

"They said that?"

"They did tell me so. All three of them. I wouldn't listen."

"Well, it's in poor taste to point that out now."

She couldn't help but smile at that. It was nice to have someone on her side, even if he probably wasn't serious. "You know my family. Nothing's off-limits."

"So, what happened with…" he paused, as if straining his memory for a name.

"Tom. Your mom already told you the story, right?"

"I've only heard the highlights."

"There's not much to tell. He's not an animal

or anything. He just wrote that he didn't think we were right for each other."

"You weren't if he could give up so easily."

"I guess, but he could have timed the breakup better."

Matthew took a long drink of his coffee before he spoke again. "There's never a good time for a breakup, but I'll tell you this. Any breakup before the wedding is better than one that comes after it."

His words made her heart ache for him, a strange feeling since she'd spent much of her time lately feeling sorry for herself. "I'm sorry about your divorce."

"That's ancient history," he said with a shrug. "We were talking about you here."

"Were we?"

He gave her an exaggerated frown. "I was trying. Now let me do this again. Do you think there's a chance for a reconciliation?"

His serious expression kept her from continuing the joke. "I don't think so. It's been twenty-one days since I received the letter, and he hasn't called. Not to return the boxes of clothes I'd already sent to his apartment or even to get the receipt for the wedding bands."

"Twenty-one days exactly?" He gave her a knowing look.

"I've been keeping count, but not for the reason

you're thinking. It's been three weeks since I had to start my life over."

Because he appeared skeptical, she continued to emphasize her point. "I haven't told anyone else this, but I was having some serious cold feet before I received that letter. I thought it was normal jitters, and everything would be fine as soon as the wedding rings were on."

"Why didn't you tell your mother or sisters that?"

"They didn't ask."

Matthew nodded, though they both knew he hadn't asked, either. He collected the coffee carafe and poured each of them another cup. Haley wasn't sure why, but he had just become her sounding board, someone who was concerned but not so entrenched in her life as to lose his objectivity.

"Even though you were questioning the marriage, would you still have gone ahead with it if Tom hadn't canceled?"

"Probably." How ridiculous that idea sounded to her now.

"Why?"

At his incredulous tone, Haley chuckled without humor.

"Pitiful, isn't it? I thought I was finally doing something that my family could support. I was so convinced that they were pleased with my decision that I couldn't even hear their warnings. Believe it or not, they haven't always agreed with my decisions."

"Really? I hadn't heard."

When she smiled this time, he smiled back, and she felt the connection only years could form. That was the thing about having longtime friends: they didn't have to start with drawn-out introductions. He already knew many of the complexities of the Scott family, and she knew just as many about the Warrens.

"I don't know about you, but I think Tom was a smart guy for sending you that letter," he told her.

"That makes five people, if you include my mother, your mother and my sisters."

"And you'll make six, eventually."

She shrugged as she twirled her spoon on the table. "So there you have it. If you don't already pity me for getting dumped only days from the altar, then I have to earn pity points for being so willing to settle."

"Why would I pity you? You put yourself out there. You took a risk—a misguided one, perhaps—but still a risk."

"Just another of my erratic decisions."

"Don't say that," he told her. "Taking a chance on love takes courage. Do you have any idea how many people aren't brave enough to even try?"

"What some call brave, others might call foolish."

"Definitely brave." He must have read the shock on her face because he continued, "You were always brave. Even at fourteen."

"If you're talking about what I think you're talking about, I need to cover my head with a bag. I'm about to turn ten shades of red."

"I am, but you don't need the bag. We're grown-ups now." He paused as if trying to recall the memory she'd relived more times than she should have lately. "I was supposed to be so much older as a nineteen-year-old college sophomore. Streetwise. But I knew as much about male-female relationships as you did. Less."

"Are you serious?" True to her prediction, her cheeks heated, but her eyes had to be wide now, too.

"Dumbfounded. That has to be the only word I can use to describe how I felt when you cornered me and…er…said what you said. You caught me off guard."

For some reason, she felt relieved that he hadn't repeated her young declaration of love now. They both knew what she'd said, and she didn't need to hear it again. "You know me, spontaneous to a fault."

"I just wanted you to know that I'm sorry for what happened that day."

"It was a long time ago," she began, but curiosity made her pause. "Why are you sorry?"

"For treating you like a little girl when I told you I only thought of you as a friend. It was callous. I handled the whole situation badly and humiliated you."

"Well, I was a little girl. It just took me some time to realize that." She lifted her shoulder and lowered it.

She was no longer a child. Neither of them was. A couple of lifetimes had passed since that night: a failed marriage and a child on his side, a close call on a marriage that was likely doomed to failure on hers.

Their cups empty and the hour late, Matthew loaded the dishes into the dishwasher and saw her to the door.

As reluctant as she'd been, Haley was glad she'd shared with Matthew about her breakup. She still couldn't believe they'd also spoken openly about the night she'd never talked about with anyone in the nine years since it happened. The past seemed to have less power over her when she didn't hold the memories so close like secrets.

Matthew had even opened up a little about his marriage, something that had to be a rarity. At least she'd let him know she was willing to listen. Maybe it would be good for him to share, as well.

She had known Matthew in a variety of ways through the years: as the older boy who'd picked her up when she'd fallen off the swing, as the mature college student who had been embarrassed by her childish infatuation for him, even as the old friend of the family who didn't quite approve of her. Tonight she'd felt differently with him than she'd ever felt before. He'd treated her as an equal…and a friend.

Thursday evening as she stood at the sink, Haley dropped a tiny yellow pill into the wide-mouth glass containing vinegar and watched while the water took on a bright, lemony hue. She set it next to glasses containing purple and orange dyes and started with the next color, which she imagined would be a bird-egg blue when it stopped fizzing.

At the stove, Matthew was just pulling off a pan containing a dozen hard-boiled eggs, ready for their transformation into edible Easter decorations. Haley moved her glasses down the counter and made room for him to cool the eggs by rinsing them in the sink.

"You about ready with those?" he asked as he turned on the faucet.

"Just a few more to do."

"This is my first time to color Easter eggs," Elizabeth announced.

"I'd heard that," Haley said with a grin. The child had been broadcasting that fact on half hour intervals all day long. "This is pretty exciting, isn't it?"

"She's dying to start dyeing." Matthew chuckled over his own joke.

His daughter looked at him with a blank stare that made him laugh even harder. Though Elizabeth hadn't been impressed with her father's rare attempt at humor, Haley couldn't help smiling. This was a side of Matthew she'd never met before, a side she liked a lot.

How strange that she'd always thought she knew him so well, and yet lately it seemed as if she was meeting him for the first time.

With progress not happening as quickly as Elizabeth would have liked, she squeezed between the two adults and gripped the front rim of the sink, lifting up on her tiptoes so she could see over the edge. "Are they *ever* going to be ready?"

"Just a few more minutes, sweetie," Haley told her. "The eggs still need to cool before you can use the wax crayon to make your designs on them."

"It's taking too long," she whined.

Haley supposed it was. Oh, to be four again and have her only worry be an agonizing delay to color Easter eggs. She had to admit they'd made Elizabeth wait a long time for this exciting event. After Elizabeth had been forced to endure a whole day knowing they would color eggs that night, Matthew had insisted that they couldn't start until after dinner.

Not that Haley could complain about dinner—
Matthew's lasagna could have given an Italian
chef an inferiority complex—but were it up to
her, she would have started dunking eggs the
moment he walked in the door. It wasn't up to her,
though; this was a Warren family event. Haley just
appreciated being included in an activity that
brought back so many good memories of her own
family.

"What are you smiling about?"

"I was thinking about my dad. I've never known
anyone who loved coloring eggs as much as he
did. He always wanted to experiment with the
new kits that came out each spring."

"And here I was worried that you'd mess up the
dyes or something."

"Of course not. I know what I'm doing." Picking
up two of the glasses, she carried them to the table.

He grabbed two more glasses and followed her.
"That's a good thing because I don't."

Elizabeth scrambled into one of the chairs and
settled on her knees. "Is it time yet, Daddy?"

"Almost," he said.

His gaze met Haley's as she glanced back over
her shoulder. He lifted an eyebrow, seeming to
ask her if she wanted to take the lead on the
project. Was that why he had invited her to join
them?

She chewed her lip. This wasn't how it was

supposed to work. She hadn't come tonight with her special activity bag to entertain Elizabeth. This was Matthew's event with his child, and he deserved to get to be the hero in it.

She leaned close to him as she carried the remaining colors to the table. "Just wing it," she whispered. "That's what my dad did."

Matthew nodded and then headed back to the sink where he placed the eggs into an empty carton. Haley's admission that her dad hadn't been perfect seemed to give him permission to enjoy the activity without grading himself.

"How did your dad end up in charge of that activity, anyway? Didn't your mom handle the holidays? I know my mom's Christmas celebrations are the stuff that legends are made of. Or maybe cautionary tales."

Haley guessed there was a funny story behind that comment, but she didn't ask this time. A certain four-year-old was counting on them to stick with the topic at hand. "Mom hated the mess that the eggs made, so dad took on the project every year and cleaned it up himself."

"Your mom was right about that. It can get messy, but I'm certain Elizabeth will be careful. If we follow her example, we'll be just fine."

"Oh, I'll be careful, Daddy."

He returned to the table carrying the eggs, the wire tool used to lower eggs into the water mixtures and the cardboard stand where the colored eggs would dry.

Soon they were taking turns drawing stripes and dots on eggshells with the wax crayon. Matthew even played the artist when Elizabeth asked him to draw a big-eared mouse on one of them. What the mouse had to do with Easter, Haley wasn't sure, but the child was insistent that she needed it.

After the preparation work on the first six eggs was complete, they began dunking them in the glasses of dye. Really, Matthew did all of the dunking, but he allowed Elizabeth to stir the colored water around once the egg was in it. Haley tried to remain an observer of the activity, present and engaged but not quite a part of the action.

"Can we do one with Jesus on the cross?" Instead of waiting for her father's answer, Elizabeth turned to Haley and said importantly, "Easter is when Jesus came to life again after he died on the cross. It isn't about the Easter Bunny."

"Wow, that's pretty big of you to already know that." As usual, the precocious preschooler had amazed Haley, but she recognized the child hadn't gained the knowledge in a vacuum. "Who taught you those important things?"

"Daddy and Grammy."

"Well, it sounds like they're very good

teachers." She caught Matthew's gaze and smiled. He seemed pleased by her compliment. Maybe she'd been wrong in her assumptions about Matthew's faith. Just because he experienced it differently didn't mean he missed feeling joy in his faith. How could he not when he'd made such an effort to instill his beliefs in his child?

"Daddy, Miss Haley says it's okay that we still play pretend about the Easter Bunny."

Haley straightened in her seat, that sinking sense that she'd messed up again settling in her gut. Yes, she'd said something to that effect, but they were talking about Easter baskets. She wasn't making any personal faith statement, but her words had come back to bite her, anyway. She braced her hand on the edge of the table and waited for another of Matthew's criticisms.

But Matthew, who had grabbed another egg and was drawing on it with a wax crayon, only looked up casually. "Well, she's right. Pretending is just for fun."

Haley wished she could hide her face, which felt too warm not to be red. His approval warmed her heart in a way she couldn't explain. It signaled not only that he thought she was doing a good job but that he understood just how important his daughter had become to her.

The remaining eggs, Elizabeth decided, didn't need pictures on them at all. She dunked them in multiple colors instead. "Hey, Daddy. Can we use these for the Easter egg hunt at Grammy's?"

"We could, but don't you usually like the kind of eggs that Grammy hides better? You know the plastic kind with candy and little toys in them. It's up to you." He gave an exaggerated shrug.

The child appeared to ponder for a few seconds and then said, "We can have Grammy's kind."

He turned to Haley. "Mom always hosts Easter dinner, and she puts on an Easter egg hunt just for Elizabeth."

"That's cool," Haley said when she turned to Elizabeth. "That means you get all the eggs."

"Until there are other grandchildren, which, if you know my brothers, won't be for a while."

He was probably right, Haley decided. Dylan didn't seem all that interested in dating right now, and Logan would have a hard time picking just one woman from his collection of dates. She didn't know where Matthew stood on the issue, and it would be in her best interest not to ask. She shouldn't start creating hearth-and-home fantasies about Matthew and her again.

Needing a distraction, Haley turned to Elizabeth. While the two adults had been talking, she was now carefully transporting eggs one by one from the drying box to their original carton.

Across the table, Matthew was studying his

daughter. "Are you sad because you chose to have other kinds of eggs at Grammy's?"

Elizabeth nodded, touching one of the colorful shells.

"Don't worry. You may have both kinds of eggs there. We'll keep these in the refrigerator until Sunday, and then after church we'll put them in an Easter basket and take them to eat at Grammy's."

"Eat?" Her eyes went wide with shocked horror. "We can't eat them."

"Of course, we can, silly." He reached over and tugged one of her braids. "That's what you're *supposed* to do with Easter eggs. Some kinds of art you just look at, but this kind of art you eat."

Her eyes were already brimming with tears again, but she blinked them back. "Really?"

"Really." He nodded for emphasis. "We'll put them in the basket and make sure everybody gets to see all the pretty colors and decorations first."

"Even Grammy and Grandma Trina and Uncle Dylan and Uncle Logan."

Probably only them, Haley wanted to say, but she kept it to herself. Matthew had done such a great job with this activity. He'd had fun playing with his daughter, reaching out of his comfort zone to become an even better father. Haley was relieved for him that the evening hadn't ended in a meltdown over their art project's edible end.

"We'll even take a picture if you want to," Matthew told her. "Then we'll let each person pick a favorite egg, and we'll all eat them."

"I get the cross one," she announced.

"It's yours."

Elizabeth applauded with hands that were stained with dye. The matter of consumable art settled, Matthew sent his daughter upstairs to get her pajamas ready for her bath and to pick out the story they would read together afterward.

"I'll get to this when I get back." He indicated with a wide sweep the mess that remained in the kitchen.

"Don't worry. I'll get it."

"I didn't invite you here as a maid. You're the guest. I'll clean it up as soon as I'm done up there."

"No, really. I can be done with it by the time—"

Matthew crossed his arms over his chest and frowned at her until she stopped talking. "Okay, you may help. But could you at least wait until I get back so we can do it together?"

"Fine."

"Oh, did your mom tell you that you're invited to Easter dinner at my mom's house?"

"Mom mentioned it. She also said it was too bad that Caroline and Jenna couldn't make it back for Easter."

"That's too bad," he said in a solemn voice, but he wore a hint of a smile.

"I think I should be offended on my sisters' behalf."

"Don't be. Really."

She gave a noncommittal shrug that probably was no more convincing than his *disappointment* that her sisters wouldn't make it for Easter. He was probably no more relieved than she was that at least one Warren-Scott family dinner wouldn't double as a matchmaking session.

Haley didn't want to analyze why this mattered so much to her. She hadn't even been one of the targets of their mothers' efforts. The truth was it did matter.

She would have liked to think that her feelings were magnanimous: that she hated to see Matthew and Caroline so uncomfortable being thrown together. But to call Haley's interest "selfless" would be more of a stretch than most rubber bands offered. If the two moms kept pressing, they just might get their way. Matthew and Caroline probably would think dinner and a movie was a small price to get the matchmakers off their backs for a while.

That was what Haley dreaded most. When Matthew went out with Caroline, he would discover that their mothers were right: she was great. He would see how amazing Caroline was and how much he had in common with her. Those were good things, right? She dreaded that moment, though, because when Matthew finally recognized Caroline's amazing qualities, he would no longer see Haley at all.

Chapter Twelve

She'd waited for him. Matthew wasn't sure why it pleased him so much that she hadn't cleaned up without him, but it did. It couldn't be that he enjoyed spending time with her and wanted to extend it for as long as he could. He preferred to think that he didn't want to feel guilty for letting her clean up after him.

At the newspaper-covered table, Haley sat sipping a can of soda, her thoughts appearing nowhere near his yellow kitchen. She didn't notice him as he entered the room. He couldn't help wondering where her thoughts had traveled. Wherever it was, her sad expression didn't make it seem like a happy place.

As if she sensed his gaze on her, Haley turned to look at him over her shoulder.

"So you waited after all."

Her expression transformed as a glimmer of

mischief appeared in her eyes. "Are you kidding? I'm one of three sisters. I learned early on never to do a job or at least a *whole* job when I could insist that everyone do her share."

"Unfortunately, I never could get my brothers to do theirs."

"Caroline would probably say the same thing about Jenna and me, but I wouldn't buy it if I were you. Our mothers are quite a bit alike. Neither suffered slackers easily."

"Are you sure that wasn't 'fools'?"

"Those, too."

When Matthew glanced at the mess on the table, Haley's gaze followed his. The only thing missing from when he'd left earlier was the carton of eggs.

"Oh, I did put the eggs away," she said. "If we're all going to have to eat them on Sunday, I figured we wouldn't want to get sick."

"Good thinking."

Together, they transported the glasses of dye from the table to the counter and then started rolling up the newspapers from both ends to the center. The experience reminded Matthew of a certain shaving cream cleanup.

"What's so funny?"

"The only thing missing here is the scent of lime."

"We could arrange that if you'd like it."

He shook his head. "That won't be necessary."

As he wadded up the damp newspapers and stuffed them in the trash can, Matthew cleared his throat. "I wanted to thank you for tonight. It was great."

"*You* were great," she gushed. Her cheeks turned an attractive shade of pink. "I mean you did a great job. Elizabeth had a blast."

"She did, didn't she?" He was probably grinning like a idiot, but he didn't care. He was even impressed with himself tonight. "I worried she was going to lose it when I mentioned eating the eggs."

"Do you think Michelangelo or Gauguin would have handled it any better if you suggested eating *their* artwork?"

"Probably not," he said with a shrug. "Anyway, I just wanted to say that I really appreciated you being here. I feel so out of my element when I do arts and crafts or try to play pretend with her."

Haley stepped to the sink and poured the liquids down the drain, avoiding getting the dye on the white porcelain. "You shouldn't worry about doing those things. You did just fine. I'm sure you always do, even if you're uncomfortable with the activities."

As she rinsed each of the glasses, Haley handed them to Matthew, who loaded them in the dishwasher.

"It's easy for you," he said as he loaded the final glass. "You're a natural with Elizabeth. Even when you're playing pretend with her, it doesn't look like an act."

"It's not an act." She turned her head to look at him with a confused expression on her face, and then, as if she thought she understood, she stiffened. "Those of us who aren't quite grown-ups find it easy to relate to kids."

"That's not what I meant."

Her lips pressed into a line, Haley shut off the water, all the while looking at him with her side vision.

"What I meant was," he began, trying again. "Oh, learn to take a compliment, will you?"

"I will when I hear one. That one sounded pretty backhanded to me."

"Only if you chose to hear it that way."

"Are you trying to convince me or the judge?"

Her sardonic comment made him smile. "Both, of course. Attorneys like to win all arguments, whether we're paid for them or not."

That she didn't even chuckle told him he was losing this argument at an alarming pace. Even if he'd never called her a child, he'd told her she didn't have any structure in her life. Once he'd even slipped and called her a "girl," but that probably had more to do with him seeing the Haley he remembered than the one he knew now. Suddenly, the things he'd said and thought seemed unfair.

"I'm sorry. I really was trying to compliment you." He turned to face her so she could see he wasn't kidding. "I didn't intend to include any veiled barbs about your maturity, though I can see how you might suspect me." He glanced at the floor and then back up at her. "I was pretty hard on you."

For a few seconds, she didn't answer. Instead, she reached in the drawer to the left of the sink for a washcloth, rinsed it and wiped down the kitchen counters. "You're just as hard on yourself," she said finally.

Matthew took her comment as acceptance of his apology. Instead of waiting for her to change her mind, he took out the teakettle and filled it with water in an unspoken invitation for her to join him. After he put it on the stove, he turned back, lifting an eyebrow in question. Her tiny nod pleased him far more than it should have.

While she moved to the table to clean, he took out cups and a box of herbal tea.

"You've always expected so much of yourself in everything you do." Haley returned to the table.

It took Matthew a moment to realize she'd continued with the point she'd started to make earlier.

"I guess I have," he admitted. Dunking tea bags into two mugs of hot water, he carried them and some napkins over to the table and sat.

"What you don't realize," she continued as she

bobbed her tea bag, "is that Elizabeth doesn't expect you to be the perfect parent."

"I know that, but—"

"Do you? Really?" She removed her tea bag and rested it on the napkin.

He looked at her, not at all certain that he did know. What was he really afraid of, that Elizabeth would announce to everyone that he'd failed to meet her needs?

She was four years old. She still ranked eating ice cream or playing preschool board games right up there with shopping for a new toy.

"If you're not sure," Haley began, "I want to clarify for you that she doesn't expect perfection. You're the only one who does. You're her hero. She's thrilled when you play with her or do activities with her. Just look at the happy dance she does when you come home from work."

Matthew nodded. Her argument was sound, even if he was having a hard time accepting it. Vulnerability didn't sit well with him, either. He felt most comfortable when he was in control of his life, and now he felt like a rowboat adrift in a squall.

"I just don't want anyone to fail her again," he said with a frustrated sigh.

"You understand that you can't shield her from that, don't you? Whether it's a classmate, coworker, future boyfriend or even a fiancé," she paused long enough to smile over at him, "people are bound to fail her or disappoint her. Even a great dad like you doesn't have the power to protect his child from that pain."

"Isn't it enough that she lost her mother?"

"It's a lot to handle."

Matthew studied her for several seconds. Yes, this was the same Haley Scott he'd known since she took her first steps, and yet it wasn't. She was still young, but she seemed like an old soul living in that youthful form, seasoned by life and yet not broken by it.

"When did you get so wise?" he asked her finally.

"When my life changed in the time it took to read a 'Dear Jane' letter."

"Probably long before that," he couldn't help saying.

During all the time Matthew had been getting to know Haley again, he'd been impressed by her restraint in not asking about his failed marriage. She hadn't even asked on the night when he'd nearly spilled his guts all on his own. Maybe her mother had warned her that the subject was off-limits, or maybe her own wounds were too fresh for her to wish to share anyone else's. He'd never wanted to give all the gory details, anyway.

But now he found he wanted to share it with her, to let her see that others had faced unimaginable pain and had come out the other side, if not whole, then at least patched up.

"Why haven't you ever asked me about Stacey?"

"It wasn't my business."

"That's fair. I probably would have told you that if you'd asked."

"I know. Anyway, I appreciated you not forcing me to talk about Tom right after the breakup, and I wanted to return the favor. I figured you would talk about it when you were ready."

He tilted his head to the side. "So you don't want to know?"

"I want to know."

Haley tried not to look too eager. She'd been waiting a long time to hear this story, at least the part of it only Matthew could relate, and she didn't want him to reconsider telling her.

For several long seconds, he said nothing. He took on a faraway expression, as if he had to relive it all in order to discuss it. She almost told him she didn't want to know after all. She didn't want to make him experience that pain again just so she could know his story.

"Do you realize that you're the only member of the Scott family who didn't attend my wedding? Even your dad was there."

Okay, this wasn't the way she would have broached the subject, but then it wasn't her story to tell.

"I guess I did know that." She remembered

coming up with an elaborate but true excuse so she didn't have to attend the event with her family. There were limits on how much humiliation a person could withstand, and that wedding would have put her over her threshold.

"I remember noticing that you weren't there, and I felt badly that you didn't come."

"Really? You noticed? You didn't hear about it from your mother or brothers later?"

She couldn't bring herself to ask why he'd felt badly, just as he didn't ask her why she hadn't come. They both knew why. It probably had sounded like a lame excuse then because it felt even sillier now. What had happened between them had been so far under the bridge that it could have traveled to the ocean by then, and still she hadn't been able to face him. She'd never considered that he would have been aware of her absence, let alone been bothered by it.

"No, I noticed." He nodded as if to affirm what he'd said. "It's strange the things you focus on at your wedding. Like people who crash the reception or people who RSVP and then don't show up. Never the important things like whether you should be getting married at all."

She didn't know how to answer that. Maybe her near-marriage offered her a little experience to draw on, but it wasn't enough to have something profound to say. Instead, she sipped her tea and waited. If nothing else, she could give him a listening ear.

"I never even realized she wasn't happy," Matthew blurted.

Trying not to show her surprise, Haley reached for her napkin and blotted her lips. Though she expected the rest of his story to come out in fits and starts, after he had started, he rushed on as if he needed to get it all out at once.

"Elizabeth had been only six months old. I was still in awe of the whole parenting thing, amazed by this perfect little person." He paused long enough to brush his hands through his hair. "Anyway, Stacey probably gave signals that things weren't right, but I never saw them. One day she was just gone.

"Her note said that she needed to find herself, as if she was lost or something. She said she didn't want to be a mother. Never had."

"How could she say something like that? She *was* a mother!" Haley blinked, stopping herself before she said more. Still, fury on behalf of Matthew and that sweet little child flowed through her veins. She took a deep breath to calm herself. "I'm sorry. I don't even know this woman, and I've become her judge and jury."

She shook her head as the anger refused to fade. "Didn't she realize how blessed she was?"

For a few seconds, Matthew only watched her,

and then he smiled. "Are you sure you want to hear the rest of this? Your blood pressure might not be able to take it."

"I can handle it," she said, frowning. He was kidding her; she recognized that. But he also seemed pleased to have her as a champion.

"Well, I didn't hear from Stacey until six months later. That contact came in the form of divorce papers. She didn't even come to the hearing. She didn't ask for any of our possessions or any visitation with Elizabeth." He shrugged. "My attorney told me it was the most civil divorce she'd ever handled. Stacey just wanted out."

"So that's it?"

"In an ugly nutshell, I guess it is."

That couldn't be all when there was so much more she wanted to know. Did he still miss his former wife? Did he still love her, even after all she'd done and all this time had passed? It had only been a few weeks for her, and yet she no longer knew what she thought about Tom. What did that say about the feelings she'd had for him in the first place?

When she looked up from her hands, Matthew was watching her, as if he expected her to have some sort of reaction. Was he thinking she would pity him now? Why would he ever think that? He'd coped so well and was doing an amazing job of parenting Elizabeth all on his own. He'd handled the situation so much better than she would have if she'd been the one left to fend for herself and a child.

"It's not the kind of story I should share if I ever plan to date again, is it? It doesn't make me come off sounding like a pillar of strength or anything."

He laughed at his joke that was anything but funny, but Haley didn't join him. For one thing, he had no idea how appealing a handsome single dad could be to single women. If while he was growing up he'd watched any TV sitcoms instead of always cramming his nose in a book, he would know that.

"There's nothing you want to say?" he prompted again.

Of course, there was. Only Haley wasn't sure he was ready to hear it. He'd admitted a lot to her today, but there were other things he hadn't said. This might not be the time to prod him for more, but she sensed there would never be a good time.

"Did it seem like déjà vu when your wife left you?"

His gaze narrowed, and his Adam's apple bobbed. "What do you mean?" he asked, though it was apparent he understood what she was asking.

"Not too long ago, you said that you'd wanted your life to turn out differently than someone else's. You meant your mother's life, right?" She waited for an answer, but from his hard stare, she sensed she wouldn't get it. He hadn't invited her into this part of his story, and she could see that he resented the intrusion. Still, she ignored the warning bells, hoping it would help him to talk about the past.

"I was little when your dad left, but I have memories of some of it," she continued. She could still remember Elliot Warren, the lanky man who seemed friendly enough when he was around but who often didn't show up to family events. "The divorce was hardest on you, wasn't it?"

"Why do you say that?"

He'd answered her question with another question rather than to deny what she'd said was true. She noted it, but she didn't call him on it. "Your mom leaned on you an awful lot, even before the divorce, but that first time we saw you guys afterward, she did it even more."

"You remember that?" He waited until her nod before he continued. "She called me the 'man of the house.' I was fourteen years old. Nowhere near a man."

"You had to grow up fast."

He made an affirmative sound in his throat.

"Do you hear from your dad at all?"

"I received a card when I graduated from law

school. Not even a card when I was married or when Elizabeth was born."

Haley nodded. Having had such warm memories of her own father, she couldn't imagine the empty place that kind of parental absence could create.

"You didn't want Elizabeth to ever know pain like you felt after your father's desertion." The last she didn't even pose as a question. She knew it was true.

"A lot of good all my plans did. History repeated itself, and there wasn't a thing I could do about it."

Haley's heart squeezed at his words. She could only imagine how powerless Matthew had felt in both situations. Even as a boy, he'd always been compassionate toward any weakness in others, but he couldn't tolerate it in himself. "You couldn't be held responsible for what your ex did any more than you could for your father's actions. They made their own choices, and they have to deal with the consequences."

"With Stacey, I should have known better. I should have—"

Haley shook her head to cut off his argument. "Would you really have done anything differently? You loved her, right? So you still would have married her. The rest…just happened."

He appeared to ruminate on her words, weighing their merit. "I wouldn't take it back, I guess. I got Elizabeth out of the bargain, and I wouldn't trade her for anything."

"Me, neither."

She smiled at him. Despite all the personal information he'd shared, Matthew smiled back. No matter what their differences on other subjects, they could always agree on his daughter.

"Well, I, for one, think you've done a great job," Haley said. "First, with your brothers and then with Elizabeth. You've been both mom and dad to her."

"I don't think so."

Haley expected the compliment to embarrass Matthew, but she never expected him to frown and shake his head that way. "What do you mean?"

"Have you met my brothers? Would you claim a role in helping to raise those Neanderthals?"

"I guess not when you put it that way."

When Matthew finally stopped chuckling, he looked at her directly, his gaze warm. "But thanks for saying that. It means a lot."

Her cheeks warmed under his stare. He'd been pleased with her praise after all. "You're welcome. I meant every word."

They both had been resting their forearms on the table, and Matthew leaned forward on his as if he had something important to say. But then he pulled back and stood up quickly, gathering their cups and carrying them to the sink. Suddenly,

Haley felt a tingling at the back of her neck. Had he been about to kiss her? No, she must have misunderstood. He would never do that.

Shaking away the thought, she cleared the rest of the flatware and joined him at the counter. She couldn't let her silly fantasies get the best of her. She might have once had a crush on Matthew, but he'd never cared for her in return. Probably on the rebound herself, she was in no position to entertain romantic thoughts about anyone, and Matthew in particular.

Strangely though, Matthew did seem to be in a hurry for her to leave now, when before, he'd delayed her departure several times. Within a few minutes she was in her car and feeling clearly put at a distance.

Matthew had opened up to her tonight in a way she'd never expected, and it was easy to guess that he wasn't used to sharing that way. Maybe this was how men reacted when they were faced with the increased intimacy of a close friendship. By taking a step back.

She would have compared this experience to that with her former fiancé, but she realized now that they'd never shared their private stories. Her whole relationship with Tom had been safe and brotherly because Haley'd been unwilling to be hurt again.

Letting her feelings develop for Matthew a

second time probably would be a mistake. The two of them had finally become friends, and she didn't want to risk losing that friendship. Still, she wasn't sure what had just happened, but she sensed that something between her and Matthew had changed.

Chapter Thirteen

"Hey, Matthew. Come take a look at this."

At the sound of Trina Scott's voice, Matthew pushed through the kitchen door and headed down the hall. His mother's friend waved to him from the entrance to the formal living room.

"What is it?"

Despite the fact that she'd just called out to him, Mrs. Scott held her index finger to her lips to tell *him* to be quiet. She indicated the Queen Anne-style sofa his family used only on holidays. Sprawled across it his favorite person in the world lay sound asleep.

Elizabeth's Easter basket remained wrapped in her arms, and evidence of the last chocolate egg she'd nibbled on remained in the corners of her mouth. Matthew only hoped she hadn't wiped her sticky fingers on the sofa.

"It's been a long day for her," Mrs. Scott said in a low voice.

"For all of us."

Though the words had come from his mouth, Matthew found that he didn't mean them the way he would have a week ago. Sure, it had been more than fourteen hours since he'd led an enthusiastic refrain from the old hymn, "He Arose," at the sunrise service and he was tired, but it was a good tired. It had been a great day, from the special music at the midmorning formal service to the egg hunt to the Easter dinner where his mother had outdone herself, serving ham, turkey and roast beef with every side dish imaginable.

"It's been a good day," Trina said, as if she'd read his mind.

"That it has," he agreed.

"Too bad Caroline and Jenna couldn't make it back for the holiday. It would have been nice to have everyone together."

"Yeah, too bad."

"Caroline loves your mother's roast beef."

"It's one of my favorites, too."

"Oh, really? It never ceases to amaze me how much you two have in common."

Matthew had to smile. He was too tired to avoid the direct hits of her *hints*. He hoped one of these days that she and his mother would drop their mission, but it was apparent from the number of subtle mentions today that they hadn't done it yet. The Warren-Scott event had been more relaxed than usual, though, without the pressure of active matchmaking. He'd talked and laughed, thoroughly enjoying himself for the first time in a long time.

"Can you believe what a great hit Elizabeth's colored eggs were?"

Until Haley spoke, Matthew hadn't realized she'd followed him out of the kitchen, where they'd finished their share of cleanup duty.

Matthew looked back at her, silently thanking her for redirecting the conversation. Otherwise, he could have expected to hear another litany of Caroline's many personal qualities.

"Eating an art project wasn't so bad after all," he said.

Haley grinned, and he smiled back at her. Earlier she'd looked so pretty in that soft yellow sweater set and the skirt with tiny flowers all over it, but she appeared more relaxed now in jeans and a sweatshirt. This look suited her more, he decided. Natural. Without a need for makeup or other symbols of vanity.

He owed Haley for more today than a couple of subject changes from their matchmaking mothers. If not for Haley, he probably wouldn't have enjoyed this great day as much as he had. He would have missed out, too.

He was grateful to her for calling him on his indifference last week regarding the Easter story. Until she had said something, he hadn't even been aware of how jaded he'd become. How many other significant moments in his life had he overlooked because he was too caught up in what he'd lost to see what he had?

Even church today had been different, mostly because of God's message but also because Haley had convinced him to open his heart to it.

He couldn't remember the last time he'd heard more than piano notes and well-crafted lyrics in the hymns he led, but today the message from each song touched him. Reverend Boggs's sermon had affected him in a special way, reaching a place in his heart that had long been dormant. It wasn't as if God had started speaking today. Matthew had just forgotten to listen.

"Well, big brother, I guess I'm out of here," Logan said from the doorway.

Matthew startled at the sound of his brother's voice. He hoped he hadn't been staring at Haley.

"Yeah, me, too," Dylan chimed. "I'm sure people are going to want to *see* tomorrow."

"They won't want to see *you?*" Matthew asked with a lifted brow at his brother's optometry humor.

"That, too, hopefully. But seeing is pretty important for most people."

"It's great to have job security."

Their mother was the last to enter the room, still wearing her apron. "Now everyone, are you sure you don't want any more to eat? I could warm up that ham and—"

"No," the rest of the Warrens and Scotts in the room said in a chorused groan that made Elizabeth rouse from her sleep.

Amy Warren sighed. "Well, I never." But she was smiling as she said it. She had force-fed them all afternoon, so it had been a good day for her, too.

"Thanks for dinner, Mom."

Matthew crossed the room, gathered her in his arms and planted a kiss on the top of her head. Then releasing her, he hugged his brothers by turns, giving each of their backs several firm pats.

Haley was right. His brothers had turned out pretty well, even if they did skip out on his mother's events sometimes. They were just better at avoiding her manipulation than he was. Maybe that was just the burden of being the eldest child.

Trina Scott stood up from the sofa and collected her purse. "Amy, thank you again for inviting us today. It was a lovely dinner, and it was so nice having most of us together again." She stepped over to hug her friend. "We should do it again soon."

"How about next Saturday night?"

"Sounds good to me. What do you think?" Trina looked from Matthew to his brothers and then to Haley, waiting for someone to jump on board.

Matthew jumped first. "Sure, Mom. That's a great idea. Count Elizabeth and me in."

"Oh, let me check my calendar." Haley held her hands wide, bending over an imaginary planner. Looking up, she grinned. "I think I can make it."

"I don't even need to check mine," Dylan told them. "I'll be there."

"Can you put me down as a 'maybe'?" Logan said with a sheepish expression.

If looks could kill, the one their mother lobbed at Logan would have made a good start as she stood there with her hands planted on her hips.

Matthew couldn't help but to chuckle. "He's waiting for a better offer."

Logan's comment didn't surprise Matthew, but the fact that both of his brothers had tentatively agreed to a family dinner on a Saturday night had flabbergasted him. Theirs was a big reversal from their conspicuous absences while Haley's sisters were in town.

Either Dylan and Logan had enjoyed themselves today and looked forward to another day like it or they couldn't turn down a home-cooked meal. Matthew didn't know about them, but he found it easier to accept their mother's invitation when they didn't have to worry about being ambushed with another matchmaking attempt.

He could just relax and enjoy spending time with family friends.

"A guy's got to keep his options open," Logan said, though he didn't meet his mother's gaze when he said it.

"You should know," Matthew said with a smile.

Logan shrugged, not bothering to deny it. At first, no one said anything, as they all exchanged uncomfortable glances, but then Haley snickered. A chorus of chuckles followed, and even Amy couldn't help grinning.

Although he laughed along with the rest of them, Matthew was surprised that his brother's words had struck a chord with him. Even if Logan practiced his own form of speed dating without the bell, he kept his options open. It surprised Matthew to realize he could be influenced by the brother he'd never understood, but he had to wonder if he should take a look at his own options. In all the time since Stacey left, Matthew had refused to even consider dating. Maybe he wasn't ready to allow his mother to choose for him, but was ready to consider the possibility of meeting someone?

Out of his side vision, Matthew caught sight of Haley moving closer to Elizabeth on the sofa. All the noise had apparently disturbed his daughter from her catnap because she sat up and rubbed her fists across her eyes. Haley drew the child up on her hip, and Elizabeth linked her arms around her babysitter's neck. As the child nuzzled under her chin, Haley glanced over at him and smiled.

Matthew's heart squeezed. He wanted to believe it was because Elizabeth deserved better than he'd given her. Because she shouldn't have to grow up without a mother figure in her life due to her father's fear to take a risk.

If only he could blame his strong reaction to seeing Haley with his daughter on his guilt for falling short as a parent, he could handle that. But it was more than that, and he knew it. This was complicated, confusing and so out-of-control that it shouldn't fit anywhere in his life. He didn't have to open himself to meeting a new person who might fit into his and Elizabeth's life. He had the feeling he already knew her.

Something hadn't felt right to Haley from the moment her mother had told her that they should drive separately to Mrs. Warren's home. Any other time her pragmatic mother would have insisted that two people going to the same place must ride together for both convenience and energy conservation. But not today.

On this second Saturday in April, southern Indiana had poured on a taste of pre-spring sunshine and heat all day, but Haley pulled her sweater tighter around her shoulders. Though she'd dressed for dinner just as her mother had directed, her skirt and sweater didn't feel warm enough. The chill, she recognized, came from inside of her.

When Haley pulled up to the curb, her mother's car was already parked out front. Matthew and Dylan would be here soon. She doubted Logan would come at all, not when he'd had almost a week to find alternate plans. Grabbing the plate of ham-pinwheel hors d'oeuvres that she'd been assigned to bring, Haley hurried to the house.

No one answered when she rang the bell or when she knocked, so Haley pushed the door open and stepped inside.

"Hey, is anyone home?"

Voices filtered down the hall from the kitchen, but still no one came to greet her. Setting her plate of appetizers on a bench near the front door, she slipped out of her coat and hung it in the closet. Retrieving the plate, she started down the hall. Strange how she had the same anxiety that she'd felt right after her breakup, the night when she'd had no idea what she wanted to do with the rest of her life.

Just as she pressed her hand to the swinging kitchen door, voices came again from inside.

"Do you think she's figured it out?" Mrs. Warren asked.

"Of course not. She's curious, but she hasn't put it all together."

That came from Haley's mother. She started to push through the door and confront the two women with whatever *it* was, but they spoke again, causing her to hesitate.

"What about him?" Trina Scott asked.

"I don't think so. When he called a few minutes ago, he said he'd be right over."

Haley's breath caught. Were they talking about Matthew and *her?* Had they finally found out about the secret she'd hidden for so many years? Had they changed the targets of their matchmaking?

But then the sound of running water upstairs drew her attention from the women in the kitchen. If the two mothers were in the kitchen, who was up there? Had she missed seeing a car outside?

She put her hand on the door again just as it swung out, narrowly missing hitting her in the head.

Her mother stopped, steadying the floral centerpiece in her hands. "Oh, Haley. When did you arrive? I didn't hear the door."

"I just got here."

Amy followed Trina out of the kitchen, her movements tight rather than relaxed the way they usually were. "Well, it's Haley." Her gaze flicked to the front door. "None of the boys have arrived yet."

"None?" Haley pointed to the stairs. "Then who's up there?"

"Oh, that," Trina said with a dismissive brush of her hand. If a sneaky smile hadn't appeared on her lips, she might have been almost believable. "That's Caroline up there. She decided to fly in for a few days. Isn't that nice? Just to see her dear old mom."

"Yeah, nice." The sense of dread that had rested on the periphery of Haley's thoughts took center stage now, and acid stirred in her stomach.

"Caroline's just freshening up after her flight," Trina explained.

Trying to clear her thoughts, Haley took a few steps away from her mother. She stopped in the doorway to the dining room. Instead of arranged for a big family gathering, the formal dining table was set for two, with china, crystal water goblets and cloth napkins. Tapers jutted out from two crystal candlesticks set with enough room between them for the centerpiece Haley's mother still held.

It all made sense now: the pleasant invitation last week, her mother's secretiveness this week. The two women had a plan, all right, and it hadn't changed a bit from before. Did Caroline know that she was being set up? When Haley had spoken to him earlier in the day, Matthew hadn't had a clue.

"Oh, Mom, this isn't a good idea."

Why she was saying it, she wasn't sure. Was

she speaking out in Matthew's defense, or Caroline's? Or was this a selfish plea to stop her mother's attempt to set up Matthew with the wrong Scott sister?

The front door opened then, and Dylan galloped inside, carrying Elizabeth on his back. Matthew followed him inside, carting a few plastic grocery bags, probably containing items his mother had asked him to pick up at the last minute.

Like Haley, they had dressed for the family dinner, Matthew in one of his dark suits from work and Dylan in gray trousers and a navy sports jacket.

"Great. We're all here." Mrs. Warren's smile was a little too bright, her movements stiff.

"Logan isn't coming?" Matthew said.

"No, but we have another surprise instead." Haley's mother turned to look up the stairs just as Caroline took her first step downward. "Look who made it back to Markston to join us tonight."

"It's Miss Caroline!" Elizabeth climbed down from her uncle's back and then scrambled up the stairs to meet her.

"Hey, everybody." Caroline bent to hug the child and then waved at the others below.

Caroline looked especially pretty tonight in an elegant black dress, with her long hair swept back from her face and delicate silver hoops dangling from her earlobes. Either their mother had told Caroline that the rest of the family would be dressed up tonight, or Haley's sister was in on the plan.

"I didn't know you'd be coming to town." Haley tried to keep any accusation out of her voice, but she wasn't sure she succeeded.

"You know how persuasive Mom can be," Caroline said with a shrug. "She wanted to see me, and she just happened to have a daughter who could get me a cheap ticket."

"It sure was a surprise," Haley quipped.

Matthew didn't seem to pick up on that comment, but his gaze ticked from Caroline to his mother and then to Haley before he glanced back at the women's mother. "Will Jenna be here, too?"

Trina shook her head. "She couldn't make it this time."

Matthew swallowed, his Adam's apple shifting. His jaw tightened the way it always did when he became frustrated. Haley couldn't blame him. He'd expected a pleasant family dinner, and now he had to prepare himself for a night of constantly being shoved toward Caroline.

The worse part was he didn't know the half of it yet.

Dylan cleared his throat to break the awkward silence that had settled in the room. "So, what's for dinner, Mom? Something smells great."

"It does," Caroline agreed.

"Well," Amy said, pausing for effect, "that's part of the surprise."

With a wave for them to follow, she led her guests into the dining room. Their chatter died down when they observed the romantically set table for two.

"Hey, what is this?" Dylan called out. "Where are the rest of the place settings?"

"Where are all the plates, Grammy?" Elizabeth asked.

"That's just it," Amy explained. "The dinner here will be beef burgundy for two. The rest of us have dinner reservations at the new steak house near the mall." She didn't bother explaining which two were scheduled for the private dinner and which would be going to the restaurant. The secret glance that passed between the two older women said it all.

"Oh, Mom," Dylan said sadly. "You didn't do this."

"Of course, I did. You know how much I enjoy gathering everyone together."

For his part, Matthew said nothing. He just stood there, his posture stiff, an incredulous expression on his face. Unlike his brothers, Matthew had always been there for his mother. She'd rewarded him by tricking him, whether she thought she was doing the right thing or not.

Haley couldn't help but turn a disappointed look her sister's way. Caroline was supposed to be so strong, so independent, and yet she'd allowed herself to be a part of this ruse. Haley might have been dumped mere days from the altar, but she still had more pride than to do something like that. Where was Caroline's pride? She'd been so vocal about her determination to remain single. What happened to that decision?

But one look at Caroline squashed every accusing thought in Haley's mind. Her sister's skin was as pale as Amy Warren's lace tablecloth. Caroline's mouth had gone slack, and she stared at the floor. It couldn't have been clearer that she hadn't been involved in the ambush. Haley felt guilty for rushing to judgment.

Caroline shook her head. "You know, Mom, I can't stay for dinner after all. I…"

"Of course, you can stay," Trina said, but she looked worried.

Had she waited until now to have second thoughts about her plan with Mrs. Warren? Well, Haley wanted to tell her that her questions had come too late.

"Okay, let's just get this meal on the table, so the rest of us can be on our way." Amy brushed her hands on her apron, turning toward the kitchen.

"Mother, stop!"

Matthew's loud voice stilled all the murmurs and fidgeting in the room. Amy did stop and slowly turned to her son. Noticing that Elizabeth stared at her father with wide eyes, Haley slipped an arm around her shoulder.

Matthew appeared too angry to notice his daughter's reaction or even the worried glances the others were exchanging. His infuriated focus was on his mother alone.

"I don't know what gave you the idea that you could humiliate Caroline and me by forcing us together like this, but I never agreed to any of it." Without looking at Caroline for confirmation, he continued, "And you know full well she didn't agree to it, either."

Amy pressed her lips together before bravely meeting his gaze. "I'm sorry, Matthew, but we just wanted you to be happy, and we—"

"Don't you understand that it doesn't matter what you want or what Mrs. Scott wants?" He paused, giving Haley's mother the same withering look he'd trained on Amy. "These are our *lives* you're talking about. We're not pawns in some matchmaking game."

Trina began her plea for understanding. "Of course we don't think of you as pawns. We were just trying to—"

"Get what you wanted by whatever means necessary," Matthew finished for her.

"Come now, Matthew," Amy said. "It wasn't like that."

"So what was it like, Mom?"

He asked the question, but he appeared to be too incensed to wait for her answer.

"You hinted and suggested and coaxed, and when none of that worked, you duped us. Didn't you ever consider, even for a minute, that you might be going too far?"

Amy opened her mouth as if to answer, but he cut her off again.

"Well, I can tell you this. You *did* go too far." He tilted his head back, closed his eyes and took two deep breaths as if he was trying to gain control over his temper. "I have one more thing to say. Stay out of my love life!"

The last probably came out louder than he intended because he blew out a frustrated sigh and shoved his hands through his hair. Haley's mother caught Mrs. Warren's attention from across the room, and they both looked contrite. They would have more apologies and some groveling ahead of them.

Matthew's mother made the first move, taking a step toward him, but he didn't appear to notice. When he spoke, the words were just above a whisper. "Doesn't anyone realize that if I were going to date any of the Scott sisters, it would be Haley?"

Chapter Fourteen

Until he heard Haley's gasp, Matthew wasn't aware he'd spoken his thoughts aloud. His own breath hitched, as well, as he realized with a jolt that what he'd said was true: he did have feelings for the youngest Scott sister. Until now, he hadn't even realized what he wanted, and here it was, out there, for everyone to hear.

Part of him wished he could draw his words inside again to the place where he could digest them instead of sharing them so soon. The other part was relieved it was too late to take them back. Around him, he could hear the whispers, but only one reaction mattered to him. His chest tightening, he turned to look at Haley, who stared back at him, wide-eyed.

He couldn't blame her for feeling confused. He'd never given her any clues that his feelings for her had changed. How could he when he hadn't really known himself? It all made sense to him now. He'd never understood why pretty and intelligent Caroline never interested him, but he'd been unable to see possibilities with Caroline when his thoughts had been on her sister.

What was Haley thinking now? He had to know. The bewilderment on her face didn't give him any clues. She might have been worried because she had feelings for him, but she also could have been feeling angst because she didn't share his feelings and didn't want to hurt him.

"Daddy, you want to go on a date with Miss Haley?"

Matthew swallowed as he lowered his gaze to Elizabeth, who stood under Haley's sheltering arm. He wished his daughter hadn't been present for his outburst and confession, but he couldn't change that now. There was no dodging the truth when a child was around.

"How would you feel about it if I did?"

His mother had stepped over to Mrs. Scott, and the two of them were exchanging doubtful looks, but Matthew barely glanced at them before he turned back to his daughter.

Elizabeth pressed an index finger to her cheek and appeared to consider but only for a few seconds. "Happy."

"Well, there you have it," he said, holding his hands wide with a confidence he didn't feel.

This matter was anything but settled, even if his daughter had made up *her* mind. Matthew was no more accustomed to this adolescent, sweaty-palmed nervousness than he was to asking a question for which he didn't already know the answer. He felt more out-of-control in situations involving Haley, so he shouldn't expect this time to be any different.

Clearing his throat, he lifted his gaze to the woman whose opinion really mattered here. "Haley, I was wondering if you would like to go on a date with me tomorrow night?"

Haley stared at the floor, her pulse beating a staccato rhythm. She'd waited a lifetime to hear words like these coming from Matthew, and now that he'd spoken them, she felt frozen. She couldn't speak, and even if she could, what was she supposed to say?

Shock didn't begin to cover the way she was feeling right now. Her thoughts raced, so many conversations now painted with a different brush of a new perspective. Yes, she'd surmised that their relationship had changed, but she'd never taken the mental leap to believe that Matthew just might have been interested in her.

Even the night when she'd thought he was going to kiss her, she'd convinced herself it was wishful thinking. Now that she had proof that her instincts were far more accurate than she'd realized, she felt panicked.

Should she accept? Of course she wanted to. She couldn't remember ever wanting anything as much as she wanted to say yes at this moment. But should she? How many rash, foolish decisions could be contained in one lifetime?

Accepting might be the most foolish decision of all. She couldn't put her heart at risk to him a second time, could she? The heartbreak she'd felt nine years before would pale by comparison to the pain she was risking now. She shouldn't take a chance like that when she wasn't even sure about his motivation for asking. What if he'd only been trying to shock their mothers for the trick they'd pulled on Caroline and him? What if his feelings hadn't changed at all?

Mrs. Warren made an uncomfortable sound in her throat. "You know, why don't we all go out for steaks? Just let me put these things away first."

"I don't think so, Mom," Matthew answered without looking her way.

Trina released a loud sigh. "Maybe we should just call it a night."

Haley couldn't bring herself to look at any of them. They all made the sounds of nervous shifting, but they stayed where they were as if held in place by the question she had yet to answer.

Even Elizabeth became antsy, finally slipping out from beneath her arm to turn and face her.

"Miss Haley, don't you want to go on a date with my daddy?" Her little face looked heartbreakingly sad.

"I don't know," Haley began, but when she met Matthew's gaze, she stopped again. She did know. The man before her looked nothing like the confident man she'd always known, the uncertainty in his eyes every bit as intense as her own. Once again, she was allowing her heart to control her head, but she didn't care.

"I mean I do," she heard herself saying. "I would love to go on a date with your father." She smiled down at the child who was grinning up at her.

Then, though heat rushed to her cheeks, Haley gathered her courage and faced the man himself. "Yes, I would love to go out with you."

At once calm flooded through her veins. She knew better than to trust it; wasn't there always a calm before a storm? Still, there was something freeing about listening to her heart. She would try not to make too much of it, but she planned to enjoy herself. Nearly a decade after she'd first dreamed about it, she would be going with Matthew Warren on their first date.

"Now this I didn't expect," Haley said as Matthew guided her into the Markston Central

High School auditorium the next evening. His fingers grazed the small of her back, causing her to smile. The previous weekend, she'd already planned to attend Elizabeth's recital, but he had surprised her by bringing her to the first show as his date. In front of all the parents and dancers there, he was making the statement that he'd chosen to be with her.

"Does that mean you like it or you don't?" He waited for her to choose a seat in one of the theater chairs and sat next to her.

She could feel his gaze on her, and her skin warmed under his inspection. "I love it."

When Haley glanced over at him, his smile made her feel tingly to the arches of her feet. He looked so handsome in his black slacks and matching dress shirt left open at the neck.

She wanted to tell him that he couldn't have chosen a more perfect place to bring her for their first date, but she kept that to herself. Though she didn't want to appear too easily impressed, she couldn't help finding it sweet and romantic being in that audience waiting for the house lights to lower so they could cheer on this little ballerina.

"I'm glad you like it. And don't worry. I promised you dinner. We'll go eat after the show."

"I wasn't worried." She was too busy trying not to read too much into this family moment. Trying and failing. "Wait. Won't that be late for Elizabeth to be out?"

"You didn't think we would be taking her to dinner with us, did you?" He waited for her nod before he continued. "Of course not. Mom's keeping her overnight."

Haley stretched up in her seat and looked around the auditorium. On the far side, in the third row, Mrs. Warren sat with Haley's mother. Though she sensed that the two women knew they were there, neither was being nosy, looking back at them.

"Why aren't they sitting with us?"

"And interrupt our date?"

Twisting her head, Haley looked over in time to see him grin.

"It's partly that, I'm sure, but I think they both realize they need to keep their distance for a while."

"Makes sense." Distance and, perhaps, space. Those were the things her mother had been giving her and Caroline when Trina had suggested that Haley drive her sister to the airport. The space was for her daughters' benefit, the distance, for Trina's own good. "Neither of them were in favor of…tonight, were they?"

"They didn't say anything, but—"

"You probably had them too scared to offer an opinion. The 'stay out of my love life' order was pretty clear."

"I suppose you're right." His gaze flitted to their mothers and then back to Haley. "Still, you would think that two women who'd tried so hard to set up their children would be—I don't know—more enthusiastic."

"This wasn't the outcome they'd planned. The *unexpected match*. One they probably think is a bad idea."

"It's not up to them, is it?" He waited for her nod before he continued. "Did Caroline's flight take off okay?"

Haley nodded, surprised it had taken him this long to ask. She'd expected questions while they were still in the car. "She was anxious to get back to Chicago."

"Can you blame her?"

"No."

"Was she all right?"

Haley found his concern for her sister sweet. "Caroline was fine. She was…relieved to be let off the hook. Maybe Mom will finally accept her decision to stay single.

"She told me to tell you that she hoped we had a nice time." Caroline had also reminded Haley that it was one month to the day since Tom Jeffries had broken off their engagement, but Haley didn't mention that now. Strange how lately Haley thought of that situation less and less.

Haley brushed her hands down the long baby-doll-style top she'd paired with jeans and short boots. "She even helped me choose this outfit."

"She did a good job. You look great."

Their gazes caught, and, despite the warmth that spread on her cheeks, Haley didn't look away. She didn't want to, even when the house lights lowered. She'd waited what felt like a lifetime for this night, and she wanted to enjoy every minute of it.

Matthew pushed back a few inches from the table at The Pie. "My last slice was a mistake."

"That's because you said each of the last three slices was your *last slice.*"

"There is that, I guess." He leaned forward and touched his finger to the yellow globe in the center of the table. The light from it flickered over Haley's face, framing her profile in gold. Each time she turned her head, the glow reflected all those untamed highlights in her hair. He might have said she'd never looked more beautiful than she did tonight, but it was more likely that he hadn't been paying attention.

For the first time all night, he allowed himself to be fully relaxed. He'd been tempted to settle in and enjoy himself at the recital, especially after seeing Haley watch his daughter's performance with such pride and delight. Still, he hadn't been able to let go, not with the tentacles of his uncertainties still wrapped around his thoughts.

Could it be possible that he'd asked Haley out, at least in part, to counter his mother's matchmaking scheme? He didn't want to believe he could do that, but he wasn't certain. Of course, he really wanted to spend time with Haley. His pulse picked up its pace at the thought of her, and he felt more alive just being around her, but a tiny part of him refused to give up the notion that what he wanted was unwise.

"I love this place." She brushed her hand over the checkered plastic tablecloth.

She laced her fingers together on the table in front of her, and he found himself wishing his could have been the hand touching hers. If not for the half-empty pizza pan and the hot flame in the oil lamp that separated them, he might have tried.

"Doesn't it bring back bad memories for you?"

"Funny ones, maybe."

Matthew frowned. "That night was not funny. It—" He stopped himself to reconsider. "Okay, it was a little funny. It might have been funnier if it hadn't been *my* child having a conniption in the middle of the restaurant."

"Every parent needs a few war stories, right?"

"I guess so," he said with a shrug. "So you don't mind coming back here again? There are some other places I would have liked you to try, but it's Sunday night. Most of the places that were open also served chicken fingers and a toy with dinner."

"I like toys."

Matthew rolled his eyes, but he couldn't help grinning at her. "Only you." He'd meant the words as a funny turn of phrase, so the chord they struck within him surprised him. Only you. Until Haley had returned to Markston, he and Elizabeth had been just existing. Haley had been the only one to awaken him from his stupor and to remind him to live.

"No, really, it's fine," she said, misinterpreting his pause. "We didn't get to eat much of the pizza last time, and I've been craving a good cheese pizza."

He chuckled at that as he looked down at the pan between them on the table. Only a few straggling green peppers and clumps of sausage remained on his half of the pan, while her cheese-only half still had a few slices left for a doggie bag.

"Guess we don't have pizza toppings in common."

She shook her head. "Or probably books or music or—"

"You're not sure about that. And even if you are right, does it matter? I'll just introduce you to *The Canterbury Tales*, and you can introduce me to…" He paused, allowing her to fill in the blank.

"Manga."

His eyes must have been the size of saucers because she laughed out loud. "Gotcha."

She laughed some more, and he joined in this time. She went on to explain that she preferred popular fiction to anything written by "old, dead guys," but a truth of that moment stuck with him. They liked to laugh together, and they shared the love for a child that was more of a bond than any similar taste could form.

They were opposites; there was no denying that. Adventurous and steadfast. Whimsical and serious. But it was easy to see that opposites did attract. He was drawn to her in a way he couldn't even remember being pulled to Stacey. As if his life was missing something, and she seemed not only to have a surplus of whatever it was but a willingness to share it.

The truth remained that he'd only asked Haley out when he'd been cornered. Would he ever have taken the step in the absence of that catalyst? He wasn't sure, but he hoped he would have. He got the sense that Haley Scott could help him answer many of the questions in his life.

As soon as they stepped outside the restaurant, Haley could feel the evening chill. The weather wasn't quite springlike yet, and she could feel the absence of the earlier sunlight to her bones.

The sweater she'd thrown on over her top clearly wasn't enough if they were going to be outside for longer than the walk to Matthew's car.

"Here, you're cold." He draped his much heavier jacket over her shoulders, the warmth coming as much from his body heat at having just worn it as its fleece lining. The scents of both his earthy cologne and clean-smelling soap enveloped her senses.

Pulling the collar closed at her throat, she glanced back at him. He crossed his arms over his chest, his dress shirt no match for the evening chill.

"Now you're the one who's cold."

"Could you pretend not to notice? I'm trying to be manly here. My gooseflesh is blowing that effect."

"Oh. Sorry. I didn't see a thing." She grinned over at him. "But boy is this jacket warm."

"Thanks." He rubbed his arms. "Here, I have an idea."

She half-expected him to take back his jacket and tell her something about survival of the fittest. Instead he reached for her hand and laced their fingers, leaning his shoulder close to draw some of the heat from his jacket.

"Now that's better."

And it was. Warmth and something she could only describe as giddiness flowed through her veins at his touch. Their fingers fit together so perfectly. If she were entertaining her fairy-tale fantasies, which she certainly wasn't, she might have said it felt as if God had formed her hand for the purpose of holding hands with Matthew Warren. Good thing she wasn't doing that.

There was one thing she knew for sure though: she didn't need his coat anymore.

"Would you like to walk for a while?"

Haley nodded. She could think of nothing she would rather do. "Are you sure you'll be warm enough?"

"I'm fine if you are."

They started south on Washington Street, passing a series of shops in the deserted downtown. Markston looked different at night, she decided, an architectural mix of old and new in the lines of buildings no more than two stories tall. Some of the stores had lighted window displays, but just as many were dark inside except for the golden haze coming from the streetlights.

Matthew paused and released her hand as they passed the bridal shop where she'd purchased her wedding gown and where the dress remained.

"Have you…you know…heard from them?" He indicated the store window with the tilt of his head.

"No. I don't think they've sold it yet. They haven't called me anyway."

In the window stood a mannequin wearing a

lacy bridal gown with a long, flowing train. A serene expression had been painted on her plastic face. As Haley stared into the veil-covered face, she expected to feel sadness. After all, the display promised a beautiful wedding like the one she'd been denied a month before. But she felt nothing. This was simply a pretty doll in a pretty ivory dress. Her own wedding would have meant just as little.

"Are you sorry it didn't happen, Haley?" Matthew's voice was scarcely above a whisper.

She looked up at the simulated bride again and then back at him.

"No. I'm really not."

"I'm not sorry, either."

He took a step closer to her and looked down into her eyes. His warm breath brushed her cheek like a caress.

Haley's own breath caught in her throat. He was going to kiss her. She didn't even have to question whether it was his intention this time. She didn't have to wonder, either, whether it was the right thing. Every step in her life seemed to have led to this man and to this moment.

Matthew lowered his head until there was just a breath separating Haley from his touch, but then he hesitated, as if asking for her permission. She didn't need time to consider the question that her heart had answered so long ago. In the tiny motion of nodding her head, Haley brought their lips into contact for the first time. He brushed his lips over hers in the sweetest, lightest feather of a kiss there ever was.

Too soon Matthew pulled back slightly, his lips curving into a smile. "That was nice."

She didn't have time to agree before he bent his head and kissed her once more. This time he settled in, caressing her lips with intensity and purpose.

As he leaned back, Haley opened her eyes in amazement. His kiss had felt like a lifetime promise, and her heart had answered in kind. Although she'd nearly been married, she understood now that she'd never cared for a man the way she felt about Matthew. As a teenager, she'd thought she loved him. Even those feelings paled by comparison to the way her heart cried out for him now. Her feelings spoke of hope and permanence.

In her side vision, she caught sight of their profiles in the bridal store's display window. It only seemed right that their tender first kisses had been reflected in the glass.

As Haley continued to look into the window, she caught sight of Matthew shivering next to her. She turned her head to look back at him. "You're trembling."

"It's freezing out here, don't you think?"

He didn't quite meet her gaze as he spoke but seemed to focus on a spot over her shoulder. His arms crossed over his chest, he briskly rubbed his upper arms to warm them.

"We should get going," he told her. Instead of taking her hand again, he started ahead of her and gestured for her to follow.

Suddenly, Haley felt cold again, as well.

Chapter Fifteen

Matthew braced himself as he shut off the engine in front of Haley's house. His thoughts had started racing the moment he saw their reflections in the wedding store window, and they'd chased him all the way back to Haley's house. Haley Scott in his arms. Wedding dresses. Promises waiting to be broken.

What had he been thinking? He shot a glance up the walk to the house. This wasn't really Haley's home. Just another temporary thing in a life filled with transitory decisions. He had allowed himself to forget that, to reach for vapor when he needed concrete.

He should never have asked Haley out in the first place, and the kiss had been an even bigger mistake. Both had only convinced him of a truth he hadn't been prepared to face: he was in love with Haley Scott.

For a moment he'd allowed himself to wish for impossible things with a woman who would never be able to hold up her end of the bargain. It was naive and irresponsible for him to hope for fairy-tale endings when he knew too well that reality would never shine as bright.

Worse than that, this situation involved someone besides himself. As Elizabeth's father, he didn't have the luxury of taking risks with his heart or hers. He'd promised his daughter he would never be like her mother and put his own needs ahead of hers. Until now, he'd never thought of himself as someone who didn't keep his promises.

The guilt of that followed him as he rounded the car and opened the door for Haley. She had given him back his jacket when they'd climbed in the car, so he pulled the collar up at his neck.

"You've been awfully quiet," Haley said as she climbed out and shut the door. She had to be cold now in her light jacket, but she didn't complain.

"I'm just tired."

"Oh."

The streetlights near her mother's house weren't powerful enough for him to get a look at her face, but he could just imagine the uncertainty he would see there. He tried to shake away the image of shining dampness in those lovely blue eyes.

Even now that he recognized the mistake it had

been to kiss her, his arms still ached to hold her again. For this reason, he was careful not to touch her as he walked with her to the front door. Kissing her had felt like crossing the finish line in a race that until then had followed an endless circular track. He sensed that she held the answers to questions he hadn't thought to ask.

Stop. He couldn't afford to need someone the way he was beginning to need Haley. He couldn't rely on someone else to fill the broken place in his heart. And even if he were to put his trust in someone, he shouldn't have picked Haley.

He could tell himself she was different from the flighty woman he'd always known, but just her fickleness in so easily forgetting her former fiancé should have told him that nothing had changed. He was the same, as well, still drawn to the type of person who was most likely to leave. He couldn't help but repeat his mistakes.

She stopped on her doorstep and turned to face him. He could see her face now under her mother's porch light.

"Do you think your mother's watching out the window?"

"No. Only lights with timers are on. She's probably still at your mother's."

"Good."

"Why is that?"

He shrugged, not wanting to tell her that the

last thing they needed would be witnesses watching out the window. This conversation would be hard enough.

As if she knew what he'd planned to say, Haley met his gaze with resolve in her expression. Until then Matthew had been reluctant to tell Haley the news about his employee search, but now he realized he'd saved it for when he would need to put distance between them.

"I've been meaning to tell you that I've finally found a permanent provider for Elizabeth's child care."

Her eyes widened, signaling that she hadn't expected that to be the subject they would discuss.

When she didn't say anything, Matthew rushed forward to fill the awkward silence. "Her name is Mrs. White. She's perfect. She's a retired preschool teacher who's just dying to play grandma to another child. She'll even be able to work with Elizabeth more on her pre-kindergarten skills."

"I see" was all Haley said.

"Well, I knew we were ending our month-long agreement, and I figured you'd be anxious to get back to your own life. You can start a new career if you like or even go back to school." He paused, trying to read her expression, but she was looking at the ground instead of at him. "You said you were thinking about getting your master's in fine arts."

"I said I'd thought about it," she answered blandly. "I haven't made any decision about it."

"You know, we never discussed this being a permanent arrangement. It was temporary, until you got back on your feet and until I found someone who could settle into this position long-term."

"That's true." She appeared to accept his words, but her tone suggested she didn't agree.

The realization that she wasn't going to make this easy annoyed him. He was only doing what he thought was necessary for his child, even following their agreement. When had the rules changed?

When you fell in love with her.

The words reverberated in his thoughts, but he refused to accept the accusation in them. He'd known Haley was perfect. Had he only continued to search for a permanent replacement just to keep Haley at arm's length?

If he answered yes, that lent suspicion to what he was doing now. It was both a test and a defense. He hated admitting it, but the truth remained there, accusing him. His feelings for her had terrified him, so he'd thrown the existence of her replacement at her like a shield. Would she leave now that she knew he'd filled the job? Would she have left eventually, anyway?

For a few seconds it had seemed reasonable, but now it felt only like a preemptive strike against an unarmed opponent.

Haley forced herself to look up at him, though his words squeezed her heart like an angry fist. Lips that had touched hers only an hour ago were telling her that he didn't want her. Again. Only this time he was sending her away from Elizabeth's life, as well. That only increased her heartbreak. Maybe they hadn't discussed her serving as the child's permanent caregiver, but Haley had tried to make her desire for that clear to him.

After Matthew's public invitation to her last night and then their date tonight, she had dared to hope for more than even a job. Maybe she could be someone far dearer to both the child *and* her father. It was a dare Haley shouldn't have taken.

"So, you brought me out tonight to tell me this information?"

"No." He shook his head, and then he stopped, blowing out a frustrated breath. "I kept trying to come up with a good time to tell you."

"You chose this one. And the *other* was…what? A bonus?"

Though Haley knew she was being unkind, she couldn't stop herself. She was hurting and striking back. The kisses they'd shared had been so sweet and exciting, and now the memory of them had dulled. She'd seen possibilities with Matthew tonight, but she'd been wrong. Wanting things didn't make them real.

"It's not like that." He shoved a hand back through his hair. "It was... I don't know what it was. A mistake. Probably that."

"Finally, something we can both agree on."

His gaze darted to the side of the house where Trina Scott's flower boxes sat barren, waiting to be filled with colorful annuals. He turned back to Haley, an incredulous expression on his face.

"Don't you *want* to get back to your life?"

From his expression, it was clear that the idea that she would want to stay in Markston had never crossed his mind. Haley's eyes stung with the tears she would cry later, but she held them back now. She needed to have her say first.

"Don't you realize that you and Lizzie *are* my life?" She had accidentally used the child's nickname again, but at this point, she didn't care. "The only life I want."

Seeing the surprise in his expression stung Haley's spirit. After tonight, could he still not know how she felt about him? How much she cared for both of them? But a new realization filtered through her thoughts, filling her heart with a hopeless ache. He believed she would leave his family eventually, so he wanted to beat her to the punch.

"When are you ever going to trust someone not to leave you? If you go through life being afraid to trust anyone, you're going to end up alone someday. Do you want that?"

"I can trust. This is just about the job and what's best for Elizabeth."

Haley shook her head at him, not believing the lie he had to be telling himself as much as her. "Not everyone is like your father or even your ex-wife. Some parents hang around to see how their kids turn out. Some husbands and wives choose to grow old together. True love stays, Matthew, even when it's hard."

Matthew crossed his arms over his chest. "Your track record doesn't exactly inspire much confidence."

Haley opened her mouth to respond, but she couldn't get the words past the lump that had formed in her throat, so she clicked her teeth closed. She could say that he'd just confirmed the insecurity she'd accused him of, but it wouldn't have made any difference. The truth was out now, maybe the whole truth, and nothing could have hurt her more. The problem wasn't that Matthew couldn't trust anyone. The retired teacher seemed to have his trust without even earning it. He simply couldn't trust *her.*

"Look, I didn't mean that," Matthew began, but she shook her head to stop him.

"Yes, you did."

And the fact that he did hurt even more. Hugging herself against the wind that suddenly felt cooler, Haley remembered how confident she'd felt knowing that Matthew counted on her to care for his precious child. Finally, someone had put his trust in her, without expecting her to fail. Now she realized that he'd never trusted her at all. More than that, she knew now that as much as she'd longed for Matthew's love, she needed his trust more.

"I'm not the same, unfocused person you used to know."

Though Matthew opened his mouth as if to apologize again for saying what he believed to be true, Haley pressed on. It was time that she had her say.

"I've tried to prove that to you, but nothing I do ever will be good enough for you."

For a long time, he said nothing, and when he did speak, he didn't look at her. "That's not fair."

"Maybe not, but you and I know that life isn't fair."

Exhaustion making her limbs heavy, Haley decided it was time to stop hollering into the wind. If all of her efforts hadn't changed his mind about her, nothing she said would make any difference. She had more important matters to concern herself with now.

"Have you already told Elizabeth about her new sitter?"

"I was waiting until after we talked," he explained. "Besides, Elizabeth would have told you."

"That's true. When will your new person… Mrs. White…be starting?" If nothing else, at least she could help make the transition smoother for Elizabeth.

"She said she could start tomorrow if I needed her to."

"Oh."

He didn't have to say it, but she realized that Mrs. White, not her, would be caring for Elizabeth tomorrow. For the first time, Haley had a job she wouldn't choose to leave, and now she was being forced out.

"It's probably best," he said, as if he understood what she'd been thinking. "Are you going to be okay?"

Surprised by his concern, Haley looked up at him and tried to put on her bravest face. "Oh, sure. I'll be fine." She waved away his worry with a brush of her hand.

"I'm not sure what I'll do next. Maybe school. Maybe another job. I probably will leave Markston because there's not really anything for me here, but the rest I still have to figure out."

"I'm sure you'll do well at whatever you choose," he said in a platitude that offered no real comfort.

The wind kicked up then, and Haley shivered, zipping her flimsy jacket to the base of her neck.

Matthew cleared his throat. "You're getting

cold, so why don't you go inside? I need to get home anyway."

Haley dug in her purse for her house keys, pulled open the screen door and inserted the key in the dead bolt. As she heard the sound of his retreating steps, she looked at him over her shoulder.

"Matthew."

At first he only stopped, but then he turned to face her. "Yes?"

"Do you remember when I told you I would be here for you and Elizabeth as long as you needed me?" As she waited for his nod, her lower lip trembled. "I hoped you would need me forever."

Matthew turned away, his shoulders falling forward, as he hurried to his car.

Haley unlocked the door and pushed it open, glancing back in time to see his car pull away from the curb. The tears she'd valiantly held in check while she'd talked to him now blurred her view of his departure, but she continued to watch until his taillights disappeared around the corner. She stepped inside the house, rubbing her hands up and down her arms in a vain effort to take away the chill that was as much in her bones as on her skin. She was convinced she would never be warm again.

His house was too quiet when Matthew came in through the garage entry fifteen minutes later.

The silence mocked him as he crossed to the closet and hung his coat. The absence of the laughter, the chatter and the sheer volume he'd come to expect in his home felt like a hole that swallowed the space.

He started toward the stairs, seeking the comfort of watching his little girl sleep, but he stopped, remembering she wasn't home. Why hadn't he asked his mother to watch Elizabeth here instead of at her house so the child could sleep in her own bed? Now he would have to wake Elizabeth early at his mother's house so he could bring her home in time to meet Mrs. White. This meeting would be hard enough without Elizabeth already being in a sour mood.

Not the first time since he'd made that rash decision, he questioned the wisdom of springing his daughter's new care provider on her. It wasn't really fair to bring Anna White in at such a disadvantage, but he hadn't really had a choice. After the conversation he'd shared with Haley tonight, he couldn't ask her to give two weeks' notice before quitting a job she didn't want to leave.

She wanted to stay. He just couldn't wrap his thoughts around that. Sure, she thought that was what she wanted, but how long would she continue to feel that way? How long before she found another project that interested her more?

She talked a good game; he had to give her that.

She'd sounded so believable when she said that he and Elizabeth were her life. At least he understood that *she* really believed what she was saying.

He couldn't allow himself to trust her words, he decided, as he moved from room to room picking up the few toys and couch pillows that were out of place. He didn't want to see the changes Haley had made to his home and family in the month since she'd been back in Markston, either, but he couldn't escape them.

In the kitchen, the refrigerator door was decorated with the construction-paper Easter bunny and the abstract potato painting Elizabeth had made with Haley just last week. The living room was spotless now, but he could still picture the mess when he'd arrived home to see Haley and Elizabeth sprawled on the floor playing with dolls. He would never be able to look at the dining table again without having the urge to get a close shave.

She might have made her mark here, but he knew, no matter what she'd said, she would never stay. Just tonight she'd confirmed his suspicion when she said she would probably be leaving town. Always flighty, she'd admitted she didn't know what to do with her life now.

Didn't that justify his worries? He'd known she would leave eventually. He couldn't be wrong trying to protect his daughter from the pain of that. He couldn't be wrong to act first instead of waiting for that pain to come.

Finally giving up his pacing from room to room, Matthew went to his bedroom and climbed under the covers. But though he closed his eyes, he couldn't shut out the thoughts that convicted him rather than Haley in their face-off. He tried to focus on her admission that she was leaving, but other things she'd said began to nibble through the layers of his defenses.

I hoped you would need me forever. When she'd first spoken those words that he recognized were about more than her job, Matthew had resisted them the best he could. He'd walked away. Now he could escape neither the words nor the accusation from the woman who'd invaded his world and carved a place for herself in it.

Just whom had he been protecting anyway? As much as he wanted to believe that he sought to shield his daughter, the truth hit even closer to home. His feelings for Haley were frightening and so different from those he'd ever felt for anyone, including his ex-wife. How could he act on those feelings and risk the overwhelming loss he would feel when she left?

Haley, on the other hand, seemed fearless as she took a risk and followed her heart. She challenged him to do the same, to trust even after people in his life had proven untrustworthy. As someone who'd been burned herself, Haley made taking that kind of risk look easy. It wasn't.

I hoped you would need me forever. Now those words ate at him as he lay in the darkness of his room, his eyes focused on a ceiling hidden among the shadows. Had he made a mistake? Haley had warned him that if he didn't learn to trust, he would end up alone someday, but "someday" had come sooner than he would have thought.

His fear of trusting already had cost him a lot over the last few years. Now it had cost him the woman who mattered more to him than he'd ever thought anyone could. How could he survive without Haley?

Chapter Sixteen

Haley flipped through an endless series of info-mercials and reality shows she hoped didn't reflect anyone's true reality as she lay back on the sofa, her slippered feet propped on the footstool. She thought she heard voices in the front hall, but she was too tired to go check for herself. Besides, her movie would be back on after the commercial break she was channel surfing to avoid, and she didn't want to miss any of the drama.

Would the Meg Ryan character, Annie, and Sam, the character Tom Hanks portrayed, end up together at the top of the Empire State Building on Valentine's Day? Of course, Haley already knew the answer to that question, but that was part of the appeal of watching old chick flicks again and again. The couples always ended up together in the end. Love always prevailed.

Unfortunately, it wasn't like that in the real

world. And real-life heroines had no makeup artists on hand to touch up their faces after a crying jag. She could really use one of those— the makeup artist, not the crying jag. She was good on those already.

When the movie came back on, Annie was on the building's observation deck, waiting for a would-be date, who either she'd missed or wasn't coming. Was that what Haley was doing, waiting for Matthew to finally get his head on straight and figure out that she was the person for him, the one he could trust?

Haley crossed her arms over her chest in a huff. She was not doing *that* because if she were, she would look pitiful. Her heart might long for a future with Matthew, but she had to ignore its plea. Loving him wasn't enough. She wanted, and frankly, deserved more than a man who couldn't trust her.

She must not have heard them enter the room because suddenly her mother and Mrs. Warren were standing at the doorway of the tiny family room, staring at her. Mrs. Warren looked shocked, as if she'd never seen someone having a movie day on a sofa before.

Strangely, Haley was tempted to fluff some of the pillows she'd piled on either side of her to increase the comfort factor. She should have put away her tray after lunch instead of leaving her empty soup bowl and the waxed sleeve from a package of saltines resting on the floor next to the couch.

"You see what I mean?" Trina crossed her arms as she studied her daughter. "Just look at her."

"I'm looking."

For a few seconds, Haley stared back at them, but finally she couldn't take any more. "What are you looking at? Haven't you ever seen a person wearing sweats before?"

Mrs. Warren shrugged. "Well, she's not wearing pajamas, I guess."

"Yes, she is. She slept in those last night. Those slippers," Trina paused, pointing to her daughter's feet, "she's been wearing for the past four days."

"Oh," Amy said aloud, though her expression said "ew."

Haley frowned at the two older women. "I'm right here, you know."

"Yes, you are, dear," Trina said. "And you've been *right here* every day this week." She indicated the family room with a wide sweep of her hand.

"Where do you expect me to be? I don't have a job to go to. And I don't have anywhere else to live, either." Haley reached for the remote and flicked off the TV, sending into darkness the image of Sam and Annie holding hands with the amazement of newfound love on their faces.

Trina planted her hands on her hips. "Well, I

doubt sitting there will help you to right either of those situations."

Amy elbowed Trina in the side, as if she didn't think her friend's usual *tough love* was working. She glanced at the television and then back at Haley. "Wasn't that *Sleepless in Seattle?* That's a good movie."

"Not very realistic," Haley murmured.

Amy nodded. "Probably not, but a lot of fun to watch."

"Especially when you've got a case of the blues," Trina said. "You have a case, and we've come to help you shake it off."

At first, Amy frowned at her friend, probably over her bluntness, but then she stepped over to the sofa and looked into Haley's bowl with soup congealing on the sides. "She's still eating, anyway. That's a good sign."

"She's been showering, which is a blessing, too." Trina pinched her nose and winked. "And, yes, she is still eating but only comfort foods. She's depressed, all right."

Haley held her hands up to stop the assault. "I'm not depressed. Don't you think I would recognize if I were depressed? And even if I did feel down in the dumps, wouldn't I have a good excuse? It's only been five weeks since my fiancé dumped me."

Mrs. Warren grasped her chin between her

thumb and forefinger in a thoughtful pose. "She has a point there."

"That's true."

At her mother's acceptance of the excuse, Haley calmed. It was too humiliating to admit that her blues had nothing to do with an ex-fiancé and everything to do with a man she'd had only one date with and would never have another.

"Strange, though." Trina inserted one of the dramatic pauses her daughters had learned to be wary of before continuing. "You didn't become a resident of my davenport until the day after one date with the son of my dear friend here. That must have been some date."

Haley stiffened. She couldn't be as transparent as that. "If you'll remember, I lost my job that night, too."

"Point taken," Trina said. "Still, I think I'm going to stick with my premise."

"It's 'curiouser and curiouser.'" Amy chuckled.

"Oh dear." Haley gripped her head with both hands. "Now they're quoting *Alice in Wonderland.* If I promise to turn off my movies, throw on some jeans and eat a steak, will the two of you leave me alone?"

"As soon as you tell us the whole story about you and Matthew," her mother told her. "For you to be as upset as you've been this week, there has to be more between you two than one date."

A lump formed in Haley's throat. No, she wouldn't cry again. All week she'd kept her tears few and at least in private in those moments when she couldn't contain them. She didn't want to change that now.

"I don't know why either of you would think there would be anything between us." Haley hated hearing the rancor in her voice, but she couldn't help herself. "You'd never considered it a possibility before Matthew made his announcement."

"You're right," Trina said. "And now I'm not sure why. I guess it was hard for me to see my youngest as anything but a little girl, so I never thought of it."

Amy raised both hands in an act of surrender. "I don't have an excuse, but then I've been banned from involvement in my son's love life, so I wouldn't trust my opinion."

"Hmm, maybe you shouldn't be here at all," Trina said to her friend.

"It's fine," Haley heard herself admitting. "There's nothing between Matthew and me, at least anything that matters."

"What would make it matter?" her mother asked her.

"Feelings would have to go two ways."

Haley braced herself for the onslaught of prying questions, but to her surprise, the two women let the subject drop. The tension in the room diminished as the other women took their places on the sofa and recliner near Haley and the subject changed to Haley's plans for the future.

Instead of questioning her decision to return to college for her master's degree as rash, both women were encouraging. Her mother even offered to have Haley live at home while she commuted to Indiana University, making the plan a true possibility. She wasn't sure how she would be able to avoid Matthew while living in the same small town and attending the same small church, but she would handle that challenge when she faced it.

"You realize you'll have to put on real clothes and skip the slippers to go to class, don't you?" One side of Mrs. Warren's mouth lifted as she asked it.

"And you'll have to save your movie watching for the weekends…when your homework is finished," Trina chimed.

"Thanks, you two."

Though she was responding to their clever comments, Haley was thanking them for far more. They were right; she couldn't sit around feeling sorry for herself. She needed to get on with her life.

Though this wasn't the life she would have chosen or even the one that still filled her dreams, her subconscious would have free reign in her writing, and it did give her a reason to get up each morning. It was a far stretch from what she'd felt was her calling to help raise Elizabeth Warren, but with writing, she would be doing something she loved and living life on her own terms.

Matthew gripped Elizabeth's hand as he hurried down the steps from church that Sunday morning. If only he could escape his thoughts as easily. He'd expected it would be difficult standing at the lectern and seeing Haley out in the congregation, but he hadn't prepared himself for the painful ache in his heart.

He'd tried not to look at her, really tried, but his eyes seemed to have a mind of their own, searching her out so often that most of the membership had to notice. Conversely, Haley had kept her gaze averted and had purposely looked at her hymnal or the organist every time she accidentally glanced his way.

All this week he'd waited and prayed about it, giving his thoughts the time to settle and his reason the chance to return. He'd hoped to feel nothing when he saw her again, but what he did feel was certainty that he'd lost someone he should have known to cherish.

As they trudged down the steps, Elizabeth kept craning her neck to look over her shoulder. "I want to see Miss Haley."

"She left already." He'd been relieved when

Haley hadn't been needed as a substitute teacher in his daughter's Sunday school class. He'd also appreciated it that Haley had left through one of the side doors rather than to go through the receiving line where he stood with Reverend Boggs. He didn't know what to say to her now.

She glanced out at the parking lot and then back at her father. "I want Miss Haley."

"I'm sorry, Elizabeth."

"My name is Lizzie." Her comment would have sounded defensive if her little bottom lip hadn't started trembling. "Miss Haley calls me Lizzie."

"I know, honey." She'd been talking about it all week. Still, he couldn't bring himself to call her that, even though he no longer minded the nickname. It would be another reminder in a week where already there had been far too many.

Their car was one of the few remaining vehicles in the church parking lot. As he put Elizabeth in her booster seat, he glanced down in time to catch her wiping away a tear. He understood too well how she felt. He'd thought he was shielding Elizabeth's little heart, and his own, by trying to keep Haley Scott at a distance, but he realized now he was already too late.

Haley had come into their home and had shaken up their lives with her noise, her irreverence, her joie de vivre. Before Matthew had realized it, Haley had made a place for herself in their home and in both of their hearts. Their family had been changed because of her. It felt incomplete without her.

The thought should have terrified him, but he was surprised to find that it no longer did. Although he'd made a point of not allowing himself to need someone again, that decision hadn't made him happy. Just alone.

He didn't want to be alone anymore. More than that, he didn't want his precious child to grow up without knowing the love of a mother. He'd enjoyed a love like that all of his life, and yet he'd taken it for granted, focusing instead on those who'd failed him. Haley loved his daughter that way as well, the child of her heart if not her body, and yet he'd failed to recognize the blessing she was, as well.

That was before. Haley couldn't even bear to look at him now. He deserved no better than that, and she certainly deserved better than him. The other night had been full of possibilities and such promise in the kisses they'd shared, but the door that had been slowly opening now appeared tightly closed. It was too late, and he had no one to blame but himself.

Was there anything he could do to change it now? He didn't think so, but as he pulled out of the church parking lot, he turned not toward his house but toward an address a few streets over, the one he would always know as *home*. He needed to ask for some advice from the woman he'd just told to stay out of his love life.

"Surprise, Grammy!" Elizabeth threw herself into her grandmother's stomach as Amy Warren opened the front door.

"Oh," Amy said, though the sound came out sounding more like *oomph*. "I wasn't expecting you. Did I invite you two to Sunday dinner and then forget about it? Because I have some chicken thawed and I can—"

Matthew kept shaking his head until she stopped. "No, you don't need to go to any fuss."

"It's no fuss."

He shook his head again. "That's not why we're here, though I'm sure Elizabeth would appreciate a peanut butter and jelly sandwich if you have one to spare."

"Lizzie," his daughter corrected, looking up at the adults.

He cleared his throat. "Lizzie."

His mother raised an eyebrow but turned toward the kitchen. "You're probably starving, and that mean old dad won't even feed you."

The little girl giggled as she trailed after her grandmother into the kitchen, while Matthew stowed their coats in the closet. Within minutes, Amy had the child seated in the dining room with a full plate of, not peanut butter, but leftover roast beef, roasted potatoes, green beans and a thick slice of chocolate cake.

"Don't you want anything?"

He shook his head. "I'm not hungry."

"I didn't figure you would be. You look terrible."

"Thanks. I came over here just for a pick-me-up like that."

Patting her granddaughter on the head, Amy headed out of the dining room and into the formal living room. When they were out of his daughter's earshot, she asked her son, "What's with *Lizzie* in there?"

"Haley called her that, and now she's insisting that Mrs. White call her that, too."

"How's that working out, anyway?"

"Mrs. White has the patience of Job. I'll give her that."

"That good, huh?"

"Elizabeth's just having a difficult time with the transition. She wants Haley."

Having changed out of her Sunday clothes into a soft pink tracksuit, Amy took a seat on the sofa and patted the space next to hers. "Can you blame her? You want her, too."

He studied her as he lowered himself on the cushion. "Is it that obvious?"

"I saw the way you looked at her in church. As if part of your heart was missing."

"Great." He planted his elbows on the thighs of his dress trousers and held his head in his hands. "Everyone in church could probably tell something was wrong."

"I don't think so. Even if they could, they probably also saw the way she was looking at you when she was sure you wouldn't notice."

He swallowed. "Oh."

"I saw Haley a few days ago, as well. She looked almost as bad as you do."

"Almost?"

"No. She looked exactly as bad as you do."

"I'm glad you're enjoying this."

His mother had been chuckling until then, but she suddenly grew serious. "I'm not enjoying this. It doesn't make me happy to see you miserable."

"I'm not miserable."

She continued as if she wasn't buying his story. "I don't know why it surprised Trina and me at first. Of course, you would choose Haley.

"She's like a breath of fresh air when you hadn't slowed down enough to breathe in a long time. Her zest for life and her effortless faith are contagious. And she loves Elizabeth nearly as much as you do. What can attract a young father more than that?"

Everything she'd said was true, and yet Matthew still studied his mother in surprise, waiting for her to make some pithy remark. After a long pause, he realized she wasn't going to make one. "I don't get it. Why the change of heart?"

"No change of heart. I've always loved Haley."

"But not for me."

She closed her eyes and shook her head, but the smile never left her lips. "I was too focused on my own plans to see it. Anyway, as wonderful as she is, Caroline wouldn't have been a good match for you because it would have been like marrying a copy of yourself in feminine outfits."

Any other time, he would have laughed at the image her comment put in his head, but this wasn't a laughing matter. "None of that matters now. I figured out what I wanted too late."

"It doesn't have to be."

"Too late? I think it is." Leaning back into the couch, he blew out a frustrated breath. "It might sound corny, but I feel as if God sent Haley into my life to awaken my spirit. It's as if He knew that Elizabeth and I needed joy and even chaos in our ordered lives, and He wanted Haley to bring those things to us."

"That does…sound corny." She grinned. "But it's also sweet. We know how you feel now, so what are you going to do about it?"

"I wanted to be with her, but as soon as we took a first step at getting close, I got scared and pushed her away. I couldn't help myself. Now

I've messed everything up so badly that it can't be fixed." Even he could hear the resignation in his voice, so he didn't assume she couldn't hear it, too. He stared down at his hands that rested in his lap.

"I wish I'd done things differently. I'm so sorry," Amy said.

Matthew glanced up at her in surprise. "What are you talking about?"

"After my divorce, I shouldn't have relied on you the way I did. You were just a kid yourself. I made you grow up too fast."

"It's okay, Mom. I wanted to help."

"I'm sorry that your father and Stacey left you and that your losses have made it difficult for you to trust anyone else."

"I don't know why you're bringing all of this up now." He shook his head. "It's water under the bridge, anyway."

"Is it?" Her gaze seemed to look right through him. "I just don't want your past and the mistakes I have made ruin your future."

"I think I might have already done that."

"Well, *undo* it. Another thing Haley has brought into your life is an example of true faith. Maybe you should have a little faith in Haley…in her ability to forgive."

"Do you really think she could?"

"You'll never know until you ask."

He shrugged. She was right. He'd known all along what he needed to do. He should have been at Haley's right now, pleading his case with the woman he loved, instead of coming here to have his mother bolster his courage. Well, he'd spent too much of his life settling for the ordinary instead of striving for the wonderful. No matter how much he had to lose, he was taking that risk now.

He stood up from the couch and strode to the doorway. Turning back, he indicated the room down the hall with a tilt of his head. "Would you mind watching her for a few hours?"

"You mean *Lizzie?*" She waited for his smile. "Of course. Now go convince Haley you're worth all the trouble."

"Thanks for the vote of confidence."

He slipped into his coat. His hand on the door handle, he turned back to his mother. "Thanks, Mom."

"Don't you find it ironic that you would come to me for relationship advice? I wasn't the best role model for making relationships last."

Matthew leaned down to place a kiss on his mother's cheek. "I wouldn't have asked for advice from anyone else."

Chapter Seventeen

Ryan and Hanks were back at it again on the Scotts' television, this time in *You've Got Mail* as business competitors by day and e-mail buddies at night. Although this time someone else was on the other side of Haley's popcorn bowl, her movie partner didn't have as much tolerance for romantic film fests.

"How can you watch this romance stuff all day long?" Trina reached in the bowl for another handful of popcorn.

"Is this coming from the romantic who thought she should set up her daughters with her best friend's sons?"

Trina leaned past the bowl and patted Haley's sweats-clad knee. She hadn't slept in her outfit this time; she'd only changed into it after church. That had to be an improvement, so maybe she would get over Matthew one day after all.

She'd even survived church today, with him right up front, but she didn't want anyone to report the number of times she'd looked at him when she should have been studying her Bible. That might have tested her new recovery theory.

When the doorbell rang, Haley turned to her mother. "Are you expecting anyone?"

"Not me." She lifted an eyebrow. "You?"

Haley shook her head. "I'll get it." She swallowed her anxiety and tamped back her racing thoughts as she stood up from the couch and started to the front of the house.

She shouldn't allow herself to jump to conclusions. No matter how much she had wished it, nothing had changed between her and Matthew that would make it possible for them to be together. Matthew wouldn't be rushing to her doorstep like one of those men in her movies. Even if he had no fear of trust, he just wasn't the groveling type.

When she reached the front door, Haley exhaled slowly to relax herself. In the unlikely chance that it *was* Matthew standing on her doorstep, she didn't want to hyperventilate and pass out at his feet. The sight when she opened the door made her gasp.

His hair was spikier than she had remembered, and last time she'd seen him he'd still been wearing a winter coat instead of a jacket, but standing there was the man who'd asked her to be his wife and then rescinded the offer.

"Tom?" She choked out the word.

"Hi, Hales. You look great."

"What…what are you doing here?"

"Who is it, sweetheart? Oh, hello, Tom."

The sound of her mother's voice surprised Haley as she hadn't heard her approach, but if her ex-fiancé's appearance shocked Trina at all, she did not show it.

"Where are your manners, Haley? Invite him in."

"Oh, sorry. Would you like to come inside?"

He nodded, chewing his lip. At least she wasn't the only one who was nervous. Part of her would have preferred that he only be allowed to speak to her from outside the storm door, but they still had unfinished business, and he must have realized it, too.

Opening the door for him, she led him into the living room, the same room where she had read *the letter.* Indicating for him to sit on the sofa, she sat opposite him in the side chair. Her mother, who usually hovered too much, seemed to have disappeared altogether.

Tom sat staring at her with longing in his eyes. "It's been so long."

"Yes, it has." She paused, waiting for him to say more, but when he didn't, she tried again. "You haven't told me why you're here. I already returned all the gifts. I haven't heard a word from you in more than a month, and now you just show up here—"

"I'm sorry." He paused, shaking his head. "For a lot of things."

"None of that matters now."

"Of course it does, Hales. I don't know what happened, but I developed this huge case of cold feet." He cleared his throat. "I want you to know I'm over it now. The cold feet I mean."

"I don't know what you're saying." Maybe she didn't know for certain, but she had a good idea, and she hoped she was wrong.

"I've realized I can't live without you. I was wrong to call off our wedding. Will you please forgive me and marry me?"

Uneasiness brought Haley out of her chair, and she crossed to the window, pausing to look outside. An offer that she might have considered a month ago seemed outrageous now.

Gathering her courage, she turned back to the man she'd once agreed to marry. The tears in her eyes were for his sadness rather than hers. "What you said in the letter was right. We aren't right for each other. Yes, we love each other as Christian brothers and sisters, but we don't share the kind of love that could sustain a marriage."

"You're wrong." He came to stand next to her by the window, but then he paused as if a thought had struck him. "That other man, the first love you told me about. You've never gotten over him, have you?"

"No, I haven't." She doubted she ever could, either, but she chose not to share that with Tom. He was her friend; she didn't want to hurt him unnecessarily.

After asking him to wait for her on the porch, Haley hurried upstairs. There was something she needed to give him. She ached inside for having to deliver such hurtful news, but talking to him had cemented in her mind that God had someone planned for Tom and for her in the future. Though her heart cried now for Matthew, she believed that if he wasn't the right choice, then God would comfort her until He revealed His plan.

Matthew was still practicing the speech he would give Haley when he started up the walk to Mrs. Scott's house, a bouquet of peach roses in his arms. He stopped cold as he watched Haley approach a man he didn't recognize on the porch. She reached for the man's hand and pressed something into it before reaching her arms out to hug him.

Something inside Matthew went cold. The man had to be Tom, Haley's ex-fiancé whom she had admitted she would have married if he'd been willing. He wondered now if this Tom had experienced a change of heart. Had she, as well?

Matthew swallowed, but he couldn't get past

the knot that had formed in his throat. He'd known there was a possibility that he'd come to his senses too late, but here was proof. This man probably had realized his mistake, as well, and he'd stepped to the plate before Matthew ever had the chance for his epiphany.

As Haley pulled back from the man's embrace, she turned her head and caught sight of Matthew. She jumped back even farther, her expression filled with guilt. Haley had no reason to feel guilty for making her choice, but that didn't mean that Matthew wanted to see the two of them together as he berated himself for waiting too long to make up his mind.

"Oh, Matthew. Meet Tom Jeffries." She turned to the man she had just released. "Tom, this is Matthew Warren."

At the confirmation of his suspicion regarding the man's identity, Matthew turned and walked away, the flowers feeling like a ridiculous prop in his hands. He could hear the sounds of footsteps behind him.

"Matthew. Wait."

But he couldn't stop. What would he say when he turned back to her? Would he be forced to congratulate Haley on her choice when she should have been with him? Could he bear knowing she would spend her future in another man's arms?

"Oh, *that* Matthew."

At the other man's words, Matthew stopped and turned back again. Tom still stood on the porch, but instead of staying with him, Haley was halfway between them, clearly following him.

"*Which* Matthew?" he couldn't help asking.

He looked to Tom for an answer, but Haley started toward him instead, her eyes shining. She stopped just a few steps away from him.

"The one I've loved since I was just fourteen." She paused as if searching for courage. "The one I still love, with feelings that are mature now and more real and overwhelming than they were then."

Matthew blinked. She'd chosen him. He couldn't have been happier or more relieved. He took two long strides and clasped Haley to him, one hand sinking into that wonderful mess of hair while his other hand released his hold on the roses. He felt right inside for the first time since he'd willingly let her out of his arms before. She loved him. She'd spoken the words aloud, without fear. He admired her bravery. For a long time, he couldn't let go, so he was relieved that her arms held him just as tightly.

Though he could have held her like that forever, he realized there were still things to be said. No matter what happened from this point on, she deserved to know what was in his heart. He pulled back until she was just out of his reach, his arms falling to his sides.

"I've had time to think and to pray about what you said to me, and I know now I can't allow my fears to stop me from having the life I want." He searched her gaze and found understanding there. He wanted and needed more than that. "Trust doesn't come easily to me, but I'm trying to learn how."

"Good for you. I'm glad."

"There is something I need you to know." As he paused, it was all he could do not to take both of her hands in his. But she needed to be free to walk away if she chose to. "I love you, and I always will, no matter where you go."

"Where I go?" She lifted an eyebrow, appearing amused by the concept. "I'm exactly where I want to be."

The next thing he knew, Haley's arms were around him, and she was stretching up to press her sweet lips to his. Nothing had ever felt more precious or given him more hope.

She pulled back but was still close enough to join her hands with his.

"My heart has always led me back to you. I was always searching for my place in the world, and now I know it is with you and Elizabeth."

Matthew couldn't help smiling at that. "If you call her Lizzie, I think we can work something out."

Her confused look only made his smile spread.

"Some crazy sitter started calling her that, and now my daughter has decided to change her name."

"Oh. Sorry."

"Don't be sorry. I'm not. About anything except wasting too much time to get to this point."

"What point?"

"The point where I drop on one knee and ask you to marry me." Instead of waiting for her reaction, he did as he said he would, lowering himself right on the walk. He did use her hand for balance, but he figured that would be better than tipping over in the lawn.

Haley didn't speak but stared down at him wide-eyed.

"Haley Scott, I didn't know how to live until I met you, and I didn't really know about love until I saw how easily you showered it on my daughter and me." He shifted from one knee to the other because the first was beginning to ache. "Will you be my wife and make my family complete?"

"I don't know. I've only waited all my life for you to ask that question. What do you think I should say?"

"Hopefully, yes." He switched knees again. "And hopefully soon because my knees are killing me."

"Well, when you put it like that, how can I

resist? Yes, I'll marry you." She gave him a mischievous grin. "Just try to stop me."

Matthew gathered her to him again, her form fitting so perfectly in the circle of his arms. With infinite care, he lowered his mouth to hers. His kiss was one of purpose, one of promises he intended to keep. A rush of warmth filled his heart. So this was how it felt for a man to have everything he ever wanted and even everything he never knew he needed.

At the sound of applause behind them, Matthew and Haley pulled away from each other in surprise. On the porch, Trina and Tom stood watching them, a virtual fan club. Haley put her hand to her mouth, clearly embarrassed for having experienced such a private moment in front of her former fiancé. Matthew had to give the guy credit for still wanting Haley to be happy.

"If you need an engagement ring, I have one to spare." Tom reached in his pocket and withdrew a large diamond solitaire, clearly the item Haley had handed him earlier.

Matthew started to answer, but another voice from behind him stopped him again.

"That's kind of you, but he won't be needing that."

He turned to the sound of his mother's voice and found her standing at the curb and clasping

Elizabeth's hand. The child held out an old-fashioned jeweler's box in her free hand.

"As the oldest son, Matthew inherited his grandmother's engagement ring," Amy explained. "We brought it over in case you wanted to give it to your future bride."

"How did you even know…" It became obvious to him how his mother would have known that the situation was progressing nicely at the Scott house. Mrs. Scott still held her cell phone.

"I have my sources," Amy said with a laugh.

"Couldn't let this happen without both matchmakers in attendance," Trina chimed.

Letting go of her grandmother's hand, Elizabeth carefully carried the jeweler's box to her father. "Daddy, are you and Miss Haley really getting married?"

"Yes, we are," he told her. "Isn't that great?"

Matthew couldn't help feeling nervous as he opened the box and looked at the round diamond in an intricate white-gold setting. He might have used this ring once before, but his first wife hadn't liked it and had wanted to choose something closer to her tastes. Now he awaited Haley's response to the ring that meant something in his family.

The look on her face spoke volumes before she said a word. "Oh, Matthew. It's so beautiful."

"Will you wear it?"

"I'd love to."

He grinned. Lifting the ring out of the box, he reached for her hand and slipped it on her finger. It was a perfect fit, both in physical size and in appearance. He should have known. Of course, this was Haley Scott who saw the beauty in everyone and everything, even him when he didn't deserve to be seen through such a benevolent view.

She had always been everything he couldn't bear and everything he needed, and now she was the only woman with whom he could ever imagine sharing his life.

Aware of their growing audience this time, Matthew dropped one sweet kiss on his new fiancée's lips. He didn't have time for more than that, anyway, as Elizabeth squeezed between them. Both laughed, showering kisses and tickles on her instead. Matthew hoped their lives together would always be this way, not perfect, but full of laughter, silliness and joy.

Epilogue

᙭

Haley stood in front of the mirror, checking her makeup one last time and smoothing her hands down the narrow skirt of her bridal gown. She grinned at her reflection. As it turned out, she had found a use for a nearly used silk gown with an empire waist, and hers was a more traditional use than as silk bathroom curtains.

Just three months after her original wedding date—the third Saturday of June instead of March—she was wearing the dress to marry the love of her life. As it turned out, she would be the first Scott sister to marry after all, but she found that it didn't matter to her as much as it once had.

She'd insisted on keeping the guest list shorter this time. There was a certain discomfort about inviting some of the same guests to whom she'd recently returned wedding gifts, though it did help that many of those guests from the first ceremony would have been on the groom's side of the aisle. Amy Warren and Trina Scott tended to share the same friends anyway, church friends, and those friends couldn't have been happier about this wedding.

When the restroom door opened, Haley expected to see her sisters in the lilac bridesmaid dresses they'd reclaimed from the bridal shop's consignment racks, or even their mother, who'd be beautiful in her light pink dress. Instead, her future mother-in-law stuck her head inside the door.

"Haley, are you ready, dear?" Amy stepped to the mirror and patted her hair with nervous hands. She straightened the waist of her rose-colored mother-of-the-groom gown.

"I'm ready. How about you?"

Amy continued to fuss with her appearance though not a single silver hair was out of place. "You know me. I've been waiting for a day like this one for years now."

Haley grinned at her in the glass. If only everyone could be as blessed as Haley would be in the mother-in-law department. She'd loved Amy Warren like a mother since she was a little girl.

"Matthew tells me you'll be going back to college in the fall." Amy reached in her purse and touched up her lipstick.

"Just part-time. Lizzie finally wants to go to preschool now, so I'm going to try to work around it. Matthew doesn't want me to give up my dreams for us to have a life together."

"That sounds like my son."

"What he doesn't realize is that all my dreams have already come true."

"That sounds like *you*."

When Haley glanced over at her, she had to blink back tears. It wouldn't do to mess up her makeup now. "This marriage has to be great for you and mom, having another way to connect your families."

"Are you kidding? This proves that Trina and I are amazing matchmakers after all. And you kids doubted our abilities."

Haley glanced sidelong at her. "So you're going to stick with that story, then?"

Amy chuckled and then hugged the bride, careful not to get makeup on her gown. "Well, it didn't happen the way we planned, but it just goes to show you that God has a sense of humor."

"Good thing when He's dealing with the Warrens and the Scotts."

They shared another laugh as Amy helped Haley slip the combs of the veil into her hair and settle the blusher over her face. Arm in arm they emerged from the restroom to find some of the other women waiting in the hall.

"About time," Caroline said. As usual, she looked amazing, this time with her light brown hair in an elegant updo.

Jenna came down the hall to join them. "They're calling for the mothers to get in there. It's time for the ushers to seat you two."

After a round of hugs that left everyone misty-eyed the best friends headed off hand in hand, leaving only Haley, her sisters and Lizzie to line up and follow them into the church vestibule.

"You look so pretty, Miss Haley...I mean, Mommy," Lizzie said as she touched the skirt of Haley's gown.

"So do you, sweetie." Haley was pleased that the bridal shop had located a flower girl dress that closely matched the bridesmaid dresses they'd already purchased. "Don't worry about calling me—"

"Mommy. I like to call you that."

Haley liked hearing it, too. Pretty soon it would even be true since Matthew's ex had agreed to relinquish parental rights, clearing the way for Haley to adopt her. For a third time in only a few minutes, Haley felt tears threatening again. If she allowed her thoughts to dwell on her late father, who couldn't be there to share this moment, she would lose the battle with her tears altogether. Her father was there in spirit, anyway.

The processional music began then, and Lizzie

hurried to her place so she could drop rose petals to lead the way for the bride. Haley's sisters followed her in, Caroline escorted by Dylan and Jenna by Logan.

The serious moment faltered when Lizzie dropped her basket, sending a few of the petals to shower wedding guests. Jenna followed that moment by tripping noticeably, requiring Logan to help her right herself so they could continue down the aisle.

Chuckles filled the sanctuary as Haley stepped to the doorway leading into the room. As she'd predicted, a knot formed in her throat over her father's absence, but one look at the man waiting for her at the altar caused all her sadness to drift away.

Matthew's shoulders lifted and dropped. His smile was contagious, and the love and trust in his eyes took her breath away. What had she ever done to deserve such a blessing as Matthew Warren? Their life would be filled with wonderful, messy and loud moments, and Haley couldn't imagine anything she would want more.

As she took her first few steps toward the husband and the future she'd dreamed of, a calm of certainty settled over her. *Thank You, Lord.* When she reached him, Matthew took her hand and settled it in the crook of his arm. The love so visible in his eyes filled her heart with joy. She and Matthew were so different, and yet their differences had drawn them together as nothing else ever could have. They'd found completion in each other's arms.

* * * * *

Dear Reader,

As women, we have various relationships in our lives, but for many of us, some of the closest and most enduring of those relationships are with our female friends. Some of us are blessed enough to have a best friend who has followed us through our hills and valleys, thanked us when we've supported her and forgiven us when we've failed her. I have a friend like that. My connection with Melissa has spanned the years and the distance. She is my trivia expert and the person I trust most as a sounding board.

The miniseries, WEDDING BELL BLESSINGS, was born out of my relationship with my best friend. We used to joke about having arranged marriages between her three sons and my three daughters. Unfortunately, our children appear to have a vote in this, so it probably won't work out the way we've planned. But the idea does make for some fun fiction. The relationship between Amy Warren and Trina Scott, the matriarchs in this series, is based on my relationship with Melissa. God has blessed me by giving me such a dear friend.

I love hearing from readers and may be contacted through my Web site at:

www.danacorbit.com

or through regular mail at P.O. Box 2251, Farmington Hills, MI 48333-2251.

Dana Corbit

QUESTIONS FOR DISCUSSION

1. What do Amy Warren and Trina Scott call their idea for creating arranged marriages between Amy's three sons and Trina's three daughters? When did they first come up with the plan?

2. How is Haley Warren different from her two older sisters, Caroline and Jenna?

3. How does Matthew's birth order position as firstborn play into his personality, and how does it affect his relationship with his single mother and his brothers, Dylan and Logan?

4. What happened in Matthew Warren's adolescence that made it difficult for him to put his trust in people? How was that history repeated in his young adult life?

5. Haley believes that Matthew trusts her to care for his daughter and in a more personal way later but then discovers she's wrong. How important is trust as a foundation in a relationship?

6. Why do Amy and Trina believe Caroline Scott would be a good match for Matthew Warren?

How important in a potential match is it for the couple to have many things in common?

7. Haley Scott and Matthew Warren are opposites in many ways. Do opposites really attract, and do people with such radical differences make good matches?

8. Just like in his life, Matthew's faith is all about obligation. Do we as Christians sometimes get caught up in the details of church and forget to simply praise God?

9. How is Haley's faith different from Matthew's? How does she help him to remember what it's like to experience true faith?

10. In what ways is Haley not a great child-care provider? Are there ways she is also great at her job?

11. Many parents think they would choose better partners for their children than their own children would. Are arranged marriages, or at least arranged introductions, still a possibility in the twenty-first century?

12. When Haley was just fourteen, she made an important announcement to Matthew, then

nineteen. What did she say and how has it affected their continuing friendship over the last nine years?

13. At one point, Matthew mentions that for church employees, Easter is a working day, often a time when he worked overtime. Do we as Christians sometimes lose sight of the importance in what should be the most significant holiday of the year for believers?

14. Amy Warren and Trina Scott have been best friends through the birth of their children, through Amy's divorce and the loss of Trina's husband. Do you have any steadfast friendships like that, and how important are long-term friendships in a woman's life?

15. In the story, Reverend Boggs gives a sermon on the sacrifice Abraham was willing to make for God. What sacrifices are we willing to make to build a stronger relationship with God?

*A thrilling romance between a British nurse
and an American cowboy on the African plains.*

*Turn the page for a sneak preview of
THE MAVERICK'S BRIDE
by Catherine Palmer.
Available September 2009 from
Love Inspired® Historical.*

Adam hoisted himself onto the balcony, swinging one leg at a time over the rail. He hoped he hadn't been spotted by a compound guard.

But the sight of Emma Pickering peering out from behind the curtain put his concerns to rest. He had done the right thing.

"Good morning, Miss Pickering." He leaned against the white window frame.

"Mr. King." She was almost breathless. "I cannot speak with you."

"But I need to talk. Mind if I come inside?"

"Indeed, sir, you may not take another step! Are you mad?"

He couldn't hold back a grin. "No more than most. I figure anyone who would leave home and travel all the way to Africa has to be a little off-kilter."

"You refer to me, I suppose? I'll have you know I'm here for a very good reason."

"Railway inspection, is it? Or nursing?"

Emma looked even better than he had thought she might—and he had thought about her a lot.

"Speaking of nursing," he ventured.

"Mr. King, I have already told you I'm unavailable. Now please let yourself down by that…that rope thing, and—"

"My lasso?"

"You must go down again, sir. This is unseemly."

Emma was edgy this morning. Almost frightened. Different from the bold young woman he had met yesterday.

He couldn't let that concern him. Last night after he left the consulate, he had made up his mind to keep things strictly business with Emma Pickering.

"I'll leave after I've had my say," he told her. "This is important."

"Speak quickly, sir. My father must not find you here."

"With all due respect, Emma, do you think I'm concerned about what your father thinks?"

"You may not care, but I do. What do you want from me?"

"I need a nurse."

"A nurse? Are you ill?"

"Not for me. I have a friend—at my ranch."

Her eyes deepened in concern as she let the curtain drop a little. "What sort of illness does your friend have? Can you describe it?"

Adam looked away. How could he explain the situation without scaring her off?

"It's not an illness. It's more like…"

Searching for the right words, he turned back to Emma. But at the first full sight of her face, he reached through the open window and pulled the curtain out of her hands.

"Emma, what happened to you?" He caught her arm and drew her toward him. "Who did this?"

She raised her hand in a vain effort to cover her cheek and eye. "It's nothing," she protested, trying to back away. "Please, Mr. King, you must not…"

Even as she tried to speak, he stepped through the balcony door and gathered her into his arms. Brushing back the hair from her cheek, he noted the swelling and the darkening stain around it.

"Emma," he growled. "Who did this to you?"

She fell motionless, silent in his embrace. No wonder she had shied like a scared colt. She hadn't wanted him to know.

Torn with dismay that anyone would ever harm this beautiful woman, he felt an irresistible urge to kiss her.

"Emma, you have to tell me…." Realization flooded through him. A pompous, nattily dressed English railroad tycoon had struck his own daughter.

"Leave me, I beg you. You have no place here."

"Emma, wait. Listen to me." Adam caught her wrists and pulled her back toward him. He'd never been a man to think things through too carefully. He did what felt right.

"I want you to come with me," he told her. "I need your help. Let's go right now. Emma, I'll take care of you."

"I don't need anyone to take care of me," she shot back. "God is watching over me."

"Emma!" Both turned toward the open door where Emma's sister stood, eyes wide.

"Emma, go with him!" Cissy crossed the room toward them. "Run away with him, Emma. It's your chance to escape—to become a nurse, as you've always wanted. You'll be safe at last, and you can have your dream."

Emma turned back to Adam.

"Come on," he urged her. "Let's get moving."

* * * * *

Will Emma run away with Adam and finally realize her dreams of becoming a nurse? Find out in THE MAVERICK'S BRIDE, available in September 2009 only from Love Inspired® Historical.

Love Inspired® SUSPENSE

RIVETING INSPIRATIONAL ROMANCE

These contemporary tales
of intrigue and romance
feature Christian characters
facing challenges to their faith...
and their lives!

**Four new Love Inspired Suspense titles are
available every month wherever books are
sold, including most bookstores, supermarkets,
drug stores and discount stores.**

Steeple
Hill®

Visit:
www.steeplehillbooks.com